The Enforcer

The Enforcer

Bill Swan

James Lorimer & Company Ltd., Publishers
Toronto

James Lorimer & Company Ltd. acknowledges the support of the Ontario Arts Council. We acknowledge the support of the Government of Canada through the Book Publishing Industry Development Program (BPIDP) for our publishing activities. We acknowledge the support of the Canada Council for the Arts for our publishing program. We acknowledge the support of the Government of Ontario through the Ontario Media Development Corporation's Ontario Book Initiative.

Cover illustration: Greg Ruhl

Library and Archives Canada Cataloguing in Publication
Swan, Bill, 1939-
      The Enforcer / Bill Swan.

(Sports stories)
Sequel to: Deflection!
ISBN 978-1-55028-981-7 (bound)
ISBN 978-1-55028-979-4 (pbk.)

I. Title. II. Series: Sports stories (Toronto, Ont.)

PS8587.W338E54 2007   jC813'.54   C2007-904970-2

James Lorimer & Co. Ltd,	Distributed in the United States by:
Publishers	Orca Book Publishers
317 Adelaide Street West,	P.O. Box 468
Suite 1002	Custer, WA USA
Toronto, Ontario	98240-0468
M5V 1P9	
www.lorimer.ca	

Printed and bound in Canada.

CONTENTS

1 The Enforcer 9

2 Team Time 12

3 Grandfather Problems 21

4 Drumless Drummer 30

5 Replacement Coach 35

6 Punishing Practice 42

7 Tree Trimming 56

8 No Show 65

9 Bad Test 72

10 Yesterday's Game 80

11 Old-timer Hockey 86

12 Practice Space   95

13 3H Hockey   102

14 The Team Arrives   108

15 A Happy Team   114

16 Pull the Goalie   121

17 Roofers Rage   131

*To J.P., who proves that
grandfathers can play goal at the age of 64;
and
in memory of Ewald, who really did
embroider his own shirts.*

Acknowledgements:

With thanks to Kevin Shea of
Total Hockey in Bowmanville, Ontario.
www.total–hockey.ca

1 The Enforcer

Jamie Reisberry cruised like a shark in front of my net.

The puck bounced once off the boards behind me. The centre forward on the other team picked up the loose puck and came around the net at full speed for a wrap-around.

I came across my own crease and jammed one pad up against the goalpost, the other along the ice.

Once, twice, the forward jabbed at the puck. No way. I would eat it before I'd let him get it. When I couldn't smother it, I knocked it out of reach with a swing of my goalie stick.

The puck dribbled a couple of metres to the left. The forward followed it.

That was his big mistake.

As soon as he touched the puck, he glanced up to see Jamie coming at him full speed. From two metres away I could see the Bambi-meets-Godzilla look in the forward's eyes. Jamie hit him hard. He went down like a barrel of frozen hockey pucks.

Jamie is big for our Bantam team — he's about one-and-a-half hockey sticks tall, and solid. The poor centre stayed crumpled in the face-off circle before the ref stopped the play.

From the stands some parents yelled for a penalty.

But it was a clean hit — nasty, but clean.

My name is Jake Henry. The year before, I had played against Jamie in the PeeWee Division of the Lakeridge Minor Hockey League. As a goalie, I'd seen Jamie's skills from the wrong side.

This year, most of my team had moved up to Bantam. We kept the same coach, Rajah Singh, and half the players from last year's PeeWee team. We also gained some new players. One was Jamie Reisberry.

Jamie was good enough to play AA, or even AAA. My Grandpa P.J. said he had one problem: although he could be fast, he didn't like to skate hard. What he did like to do was hit guys. Anyone who skated near my goal was fresh meat. He especially loved to catch a speedy forward with his head down. *Crunch*!

I was glad he was on our team.

On the next face-off, our centre Willie won the draw. He banged the puck off the boards, trying to chip it out over the blue line. The opposing defence on point stopped it, ragged the puck once, caught Willie lumbering out over the line, and got his whole body behind a slapshot.

It was a bullet, but I could see it all the way in. I stuck out one pad.

The rebound went out a half-stick length. Jamie tried to clear it but missed. A forward on the other team roared in.

I dropped on it, pulling the loose puck in with my glove hand and covering that with my blocker and stick.

The forward jabbed — once, twice — trying to work it loose. Then he came down hard with an axe swing. My blocker saved me from a broken hand.

Jamie caught the forward in the chest and under his chin with a cross-check that put him on his back, leaving him admiring the overhead lights.

"Leave my goalie alone," he said with a snarl.

I knew it would be an interesting season.

2 Team Time

In spite of Jamie's three penalties, we won the game 3–2. It was three weeks into the season and we were undefeated: three wins, one tie – and two shutouts.

I'm a goalie. I love the shutouts.

After the game, Coach Rajah gathered us into the dressing room.

"Quiet, please," he said quietly.

He was pretending to dig something out of his left ear. The players up and down the line got the idea. The earphones were removed. I shook the hair out of my eyes and looked up, undoing my pads. Rajah signalled with his little finger and I stopped.

Coach Rajah has black hair and sharp eyes, and he once played centre forward for the Major Junior Oshawa Generals. A lot of NHL stars have played for the Generals, including Bobby Orr (one of my grandfathers calls him the best player ever) and Eric Lindros (the same grandfather calls Lindros the best player *never*, injuries having kept him from showing his full talent).

"Guys," Rajah said, giving the word lots of hang time.

He stood in the centre of the gear-littered dressing room. Beside him, rocking on his heels, stood Jamie Reisberry's father. Mr. Reisberry owned Reisberry's Roofing, the company that sponsored our team, — the Roofers. A tall man, Mr. Reisberry had thinning hair, a thin face, and thin arms and legs that, even through his clothes, made him look like he had very big elbows and very big knees.

"We've been together two years now," Coach Rajah said. "I've seen you grow from snotty-nose pee-wees to snotty-nose Bantams." He smiled.

We all smiled back. But right away Rajah wasn't smiling any more.

"This is the best you have been," he said.

"Right on," said Willie. The rest of the team silenced him with their eyes.

"You've got the season off to a good start," continued Coach Rajah. "And you will become a tight team this year. You are now showing all the things we've been working on all this time. By the end of the season, you'll be at the top of the league."

Strange, I thought. We are the top of the league. We were the only undefeated team.

A hush wrapped the room. Coach Rajah held up his hand. "I — "

My Grandpa P.J. was bullying his way into the dressing room. Some people can slip into a room and you never notice them. Not Grandpa P.J.

"Great game, Roofers," he said in his biggest voice. "Except for you, Wee Willie. You spent most of the time asleep on the bench." Willie grinned. He had scored twice. If that is Willie sleeping, then awake he'd be dynamite.

Grandpa P.J. is still taller than me, and maybe twice as wide. He has slicked-back grey hair and a greying moustache. He is always talking, often loud, and sometimes embarrassing.

"And you, Jake Henry," he said, tossing a sports drink at me. "You looked as though the net was a hammock the way you were resting."

Coach Rajah turned to Grandpa P.J.

"We were just wrapping things up," he said. Grandpa P.J. gave him a funny look. "Just the team," Coach added.

"Just Rajah and the team," Mr. Reisberry repeated, scowling.

Grandpa P.J. threw up his hands in mock horror. He spread his arms out. He opened his mouth.

"And you?" P.J. asked Mr. Reisberry.

"Just the team and the coach," Mr. Reisberry said, "… and the sponsor."

An awkward silence fell.

"We'll just be a few minutes," Coach Rajah said.

"Me?" P.J. asked. With one finger he jabbed his finger toward the door.

"You mean you want me to …?" Grandpa P.J. repeated the jabbing motion. A couple of my teammates started to giggle.

"Yes," said Rajah. "I want you to …" With this fingers, he made a walking gesture.

"Oh," said Grandpa P.J., looking puzzled.

He made an attempt at a sad clown face, hunching his shoulders and slouching toward the door. He pulled open the door to let the arena sounds bounce into the room. Holding the door just for an instant, he half-turned to Coach Rajah.

"Your fly's undone, Raj," he said.

★ ★ ★

The door closed slowly, hissing as though someone had let the air of the room. In a way, I guess he had.

"Better check, Coach!" said Willie, and everybody laughed.

Rajah grinned, did check, and everybody laughed.

"Some day," he said to me, "one of your grandfathers is going to … to …"

"It'll come to you, Coach," said Jamie Reisberry. "It'll come to you."

I looked down the line of the benches. All faces were still turned toward the coach.

"I won't be coaching any more," he said.

The room went from quiet to silent.

I was the one who broke the silence. "What do you mean, won't be coaching?"

"I'm sorry," said Coach Rajah. "My company wants me to move to Montreal. I won't be able to finish the year as your coach."

"That sucks," said Morley. "You're not going to be a Habs fan are you?"

Morley was a fan of the Toronto Maple Leafs. He had all the bumph, including a bedroom painted in Leafs' colours, with a Leafs' overhead light clock, a Leafs' bedspread, Leafs' curtains and hockey sticks on the wall. Even when the Leafs didn't make the playoffs, he still supported them. To him, Leafs were hockey.

Coach Rajah laughed. "No chance," he said.

Joseph tossed a ball of tape into the garbage bin. "You won't be here?" he asked.

"You mean we will have to get another, totally new coach?" asked Willie. Willie was my best friend.

"But no one can replace Coach Rajah," said Bill Glendinning. "He's the best." He actually was — the year before he had won the Coach of the Year.

"It'd take someone really special," said Maurice Lambert. "Really."

"I agree," said Mr. Reisberry. "I'm expecting big things this year for my team."

Everyone sat for a moment with elbows on knees, examining their skate laces.

"You flatter me, gentlemen," said Coach Rajah. "But the truth is, almost anyone could coach this team. Why, even the next person who walks through that door could coach this team to the championship."

"Yeah, right," someone grumbled.

Just then the door opened with a loud thump, followed by a crash, and Grandpa P.J. came barging through.

"So is this team chat done and a devoted fan allowed to come in?" he asked.

Everyone in the room turned toward him.

Morley looked up at Grandpa P.J. and smiled.

"I am sure glad Coach Rajah was kidding," he said.

"Kidding? About what?" asked Grandpa P.J.

"He just said …" began Morley, but his voice was lost in the rising chatter. The dressing room sneaked back to normal. Laces were untied. Sweaters came off. Helmets were dropped into equipment bags. Gloves were stuffed into helmets. The room stank of sweat and mouldy equipment.

"He just said that the next person to come through the door could coach this team to the championship," said Willie, shouting just to be heard.

"Why would he say that?' asked P.J.

"Because he quit!" said Bill Glendinning.

"He didn't quit, he was traded!" said Frank Kennedy.

"Not traded, transferred," said Willie. "He's moving

to Montreal and can't coach us after this month."

Grandpa P.J. turned to Coach Rajah. "That right?" he asked.

Coach Rajah nodded. "I have a couple more weeks. I just learned about it yesterday. It's a career opportunity that I cannot turn down."

"Does the league know?" asked P.J.

"I told them. And the sponsor. Mr. Reisberry here, isn't too happy about it."

Jamie's father looked over from the bench near Jamie.

"It's not what I signed on for," Mr. Reisberry said. "Good coaching is the key to winning. Rajah is one of the reasons I wanted Jamie to play on this team. He's why I decided to sponsor this team."

P.J. gave Mr. Reisberry a strange look. I had thought it a coincidence that Jamie ended up on the Roofers, the team his father sponsored. Now I wasn't so sure.

"Anyway," said Coach Rajah, "I've put out feelers to find a qualified coach. It is not going to be easy, now that the season has started. In Oshawa, the rec league had to scrape pretty hard to find enough coaches."

Oshawa is a city next door to Clarington, where I live. My team is one of twenty in bantam house league of the Clarington League this year. Oshawa has a parks league, church leagues, rep hockey, AA and AAA teams, and both boys and girls leagues. That's a lot of coaches.

"The kids need a coach," said P.J.

"A *qualified* coach," said Mr. Reisberry from across the dressing room, without turning to look.

"I could do it," P.J. said.

Right in the dressing room, in front of everybody, he said that. I almost died of embarrassment.

"That's really generous," said Mr. Reisberry. "But Rajah is going to leave big boots to fill. This may be house league, but Rajah is the coach that even the rep teams come to for advice. I think that's the kind of standard we want to continue."

"Isn't that for the league to decide?" asked P.J.

Mr. Reisberry looked as though he had stepped in doggie-do. "I think they will listen to my advice," he said.

P.J. put on his joking face. "Well, if the team needs me, I'm here," he said.

He turned to me. "You know what you need to work on?" he said. "Cleaning your crease. It's nice to have guys like Jamie there trying to protect you, but you have to be your own enforcer. If someone comes in your crease, let them know that you don't like it."

"It's kind of hard when you're down on your knees grabbing the puck," I replied.

"Tell me about it," P.J. said. "But sometimes you have to realize that if something's going to be done, you better be prepared to do it yourself."

I looked up at Grandpa P.J., quietly shaking my

head. It is true that he knew a lot about hockey, and he had helped at some practices, mostly with goalies. He still played hockey himself as a goalie in two leagues and a weekly pickup game. Last year, he had helped Victoria Eldridge and me; this year it was just me. P.J. did know a lot about hockey, but he knew nothing about coaching. Once he yelled at a kid, and he gave a clinic to the team on using butt-ends and spearing, sneaky stuff that can hurt people. Most of his ideas about hockey had gone out with the dinosaurs. And often kids couldn't tell when he was kidding and when he was serious.

Mr. Reisberry continued as if P.J. wasn't in the room: "To qualify for the Markham tournament, a house-league team has to be in the top three by the Christmas break. There will be scouts at that tournament. I'll see if I can pull some more strings."

I looked up at Grandpa P.J. He had that look you get when a girl you like tells you to get lost. Or when you were really, really counting on tickets to a hot concert and your dad couldn't get them for you, even though he had promised. Or when you don't get the lead part in the school play (even though you told everybody you didn't want it).

That look — disappointed, and trying not to show it. The kind of look you get just before you start crying, even though you're not a little kid anymore and don't do that.

Grandpa P.J. caught my eye and looked away.

3 Grandfather Problems

Two of my three grandfathers filled the kitchen at home later that afternoon. They slurped coffee out of paper cups and boasted about how tough things were when they were kids.

Many people find my family a bit confusing. Some think it strange that I have three grandfathers. It's not that unusual. One kid I know at school has four, but they don't speak to one another. My folks are different. They're always getting together, even my mom and my dad, who were divorced when I was three.

That's how I ended up with three grandfathers, plus one mother, one father, one stepfather, and one grandmother. They all speak to each other — sometimes too much.

My mom's parents are Grandpa Gord and Nanny Joyce. Grandpa Gord plays the fiddle. He takes cowbells to all of my hockey games.

After my parents got divorced, Mom married Fred.

Fred's father is Grandpa P.J. His mother died a long time ago.

The only members of the happy family missing were my dad and his father Grandpa Ron. Sometimes I think I get too much attention. Take Grandpa Gord and the fiddle. He's been teaching me the fiddle since I was in grade one. At first it was on a miniature violin, but last Christmas he bought me a full-sized one. Every Saturday he comes over for lessons, and every family gathering he expects me to play with him.

What I really want is Saturday afternoons free to practice with my rock band. All I need is a set of drums and I'm ready to go. The trouble is, I don't know how to tell Grandpa Gord that I don't want to play the fiddle any more. The fiddle is okay at family picnics, but it really doesn't rock. How do you tell that to a grandfather without hurting his feelings?

Now Grandpa P.J. wants to coach my hockey team.

"I really think I could coach the Roofers," P.J. said.

I didn't look at him. I couldn't.

Across the table from him, Grandpa Gord blew across the top of his coffee, making little waves on the surface. "Coach Rajah will be hard to replace," he said.

Fred came into the room. "You haven't coached since I was Jake's age, P.J.," he said. Even P.J.'s own son called him by his initials. "That's a quarter-century ago."

"Well, it's like riding a bicycle," replied P.J. "You never forget."

Fred unplugged the boiling kettle and made a cup of tea.

"If I remember correctly, that didn't work out all that well," he said, "your coaching my team."

P.J. huffed once and slurped coffee.

"I seem to remember that you yelled a lot," Fred added.

P.J. stopped slurping and sipped. "At the parents," he said. "I yelled only at the parents."

Fred shrugged. "Whatever," he said. "Memory is an elusive thing."

"I've taken a coaching program," P.J. said. "I am qualified now."

That's when Grandpa Ron and my father walked in the door.

"You got coffee on, or do we have to go down to Timmy's?" he asked.

My father gave me a hug. "Sorry I missed your game, Sport," he said. "We've been sitting on the 401 for hours."

"Bad?" asked Fred.

"Six hours from London," said my dad. "Big pile-up. Almost as crowded as this kitchen."

"We won without you," I said.

A few minutes later Willie came to the door with a hockey stick in his hands.

My dad gave me a thumbs-up. "Fred and I are going to have our usual game of chess," he said. "Why don't you go out with Willie for road hockey?"

Actually, it was driveway hockey. And it was Willie and Victoria.

★ ★ ★

Victoria Eldridge hugged the goalpost and waved her blocker. Willie wound up for a slapper. *Barrong-zong*!

The tennis ball bounced once off the crossbar, hit the metal of the garage door, and went up and over — over Willie's head, over my head — and out into the street. It dribbled in smaller bounces and ended up against the curb two doors down.

I've told you about Willie. He's big and strong and plays centre most of the time. He has a slapshot that could drill a hole in a goalie leaving you with — you got it — a holey goalie!"

Last year, Victoria and I had alternated playing goal and left defence for the Bear Claws. This year Victoria played on the Clarington girls rep team, the Clarington Flames. Her ambition was to play in the Olympics.

Victoria is almost my height. Like me, she is thirteen. She has long, brown hair and soft, brown goaltender eyes that won't blink.

"I mean," she said in her kind-of-adult voice, as Willie went after the ball, "having P.J. as a coach would be great. I don't see what the problem is."

"The problem is," I said, "that Grandpa P.J. doesn't

know any more about coaching than he knows about computers."

"He coached us fairly well last year," said Vickie. "Remember those one-on-one sessions? In fact, it was his coaching that helped me make the Flames this year."

I hadn't known that.

"Jake Henry, I don't think you know how good he is."

"That was goalie coaching," I said. "He knows goalie stuff. But he couldn't coach a team. No way."

Vickie looked at me with those unblinking eyes. "How do you know that?" she asked.

Willie flicked the tennis ball to me from the street. I tried to roof it into the top corner. Vickie nabbed it with her glove hand — snap. I had thought she wasn't looking.

"What about your band?" she asked.

That's just like a girl — changing the subject so fast you think your head will spin off.

"That's a different problem," I snapped.

"You've got grandfather problem-zzzz," she said, drawing out the end of the word.

"What do you mean, problem-zzz?" I asked.

Victoria snapped her bubble gum. "Have you told Grandpa Gord yet?"

Willie whacked at the tennis ball and sent it to the top left corner of the net, where Vickie's blocker met it and sent it over to the next lawn.

"Told Grandpa Gord what?" he asked.

Vickie lifted her mask back over her forehead. "He hasn't told his Grandpa Gord about the rock band yet."

"So?" asked Willie.

"He hasn't told his Grandpa Gord that he won't have time for fiddle lessons," she said.

Willie shrugged.

"Sounds as though you have two grandpa problems," she said. "But I think the main problem is in your head."

"What's that supposed to mean?" I asked, chopping down hard on the tennis ball.

"Think about it," she said. "You don't want to tell Grandpa Gord about the band because you are worried about how he will react."

She let that point sink in. When she said it that way, it sounded so simple.

"And you're worried about Grandpa P.J. coaching because you're afraid he'll embarrass you. Or that Jamie Reisberry might not like it, or Jamie's father wouldn't like it, or something. Nobody is sure what. I don't think *you* do."

She made both problems sound simple.

"You should be worrying that your team gets a coach at all," she said. "That's a real problem."

"And you want to be a drummer in a rock band and you don't have a set of drums," she added. "That is also a real problem."

She was right, of course. Drums cost money. Practice pads are all right for practicing by yourself. But when the band gets together, practice pads just don't make it. The drums have got to be there, man. They have to be woven all through the music. They have to wrap around the guitar and join up the keyboards. They have to give everybody a body. They have to cover everybody else's mistakes.

Just like a goalie has to cover everybody else's mistakes on the ice.

A forward can really goof, and all he misses is a chance to score. Defence can really goof off, and have somebody dance past to get to the goal.

But if the goalie stops the puck, nobody remembers that anyone else did something stupid.

If a goalie *doesn't* stop the puck, nobody remembers that it was the forwards and defence who messed up. They remember the last mistake, the one the goalie made. Even if the goalie didn't have a chance on the play, it's still the goalie's mistake.

"So what are you going to do?" Vickie asked.

I lined up a slapshot.

The shot missed the net, bounced off the brick wall beside the garage door, and headed down the street.

"Go get the ball," Willie said.

We had a rule: you shoot it, you chase it.

The tennis ball is good for street hockey. It doesn't

hurt as much as a puck. But it rolls farther. In this case, down the road to Mr. Valentine's. Mr. Valentine is the neighbourhood grouch. Last year, Mr. Valentine had collected all the tennis balls that went on his property. P.J. made him give them back, a whole bushel-basketful.

"Hurry up and get it before old Valentine does," said Willie.

On roller blades, it took me only seconds to catch up to the ball. But it had already rolled onto Mr. Valentine's lawn. And there he was, tossing the ball up and down, up and down.

"Sorry, Mr. Valentine," I said.

Slowly he handed the ball to me. He shook his head from side to side.

"Kids," he said, and turned back to his garage. "Gol-darned kids."

I skated back to our driveway and wristed a shot. Vickie gloved it easily.

"The way I see it," she said, removing her helmet in a way that said our game was over, "is that you are missing the real problems here. You're all tied up about how other people feel, which is fine. Being considerate is great. But you can't run your life based on that."

I stared at her. When she shook out her hair like that she turned from a goalie into a girl, just like that.

"On the other hand," she continued, "you don't want to be a self-centred twit who cares only about himself."

It bothered me the way she could sound like an adult.

"Your real problems are getting a coach for your team and a set of drums so you can play in the band," she said, "and to achieve both without stomping all over everybody's feelings."

She gathered her gloves, mask, and stick and held them under both arms to carry home.

"Well," said Willie, "you could always borrow your parents' pots and pans."

I slapped the ball hard. It echoed loudly against the garage door.

"One thing is for sure," said Victoria. "You sure aren't going to have much of a band until you get drums."

She paused.

"Or until the band finds another drummer who does."

4 Drumless Drummer

Later that Saturday afternoon I told Grandpa Gord that I didn't want to take violin lessons any more.

Grandpa Gord is weird in his own way. Every hockey game he brings cowbells, which he rings every time my team scores — sometimes when the other team scores, and sometimes just by mistake, because it is hard to move with cowbells in your hand without making a noise. He knows zilch about hockey, and he gets excited easily.

He slurped from the top of his cup of coffee and lifted his eyebrows.

"Hmm, okay, then. Maybe later," he said.

"Un-uh," I said in kind of a grunt. "Don't want to play no more."

"Don't want to play no more," said Grandpa Gord, imitating my grunt.

He wore one of his cowboy shirts with little frilly strings across the chest. I don't know where he gets them.

"Nope."

He let out a big breath. "Okay," he said.

Then there was silence. And more silence.

"Three of my friends and me, we've started a rock band," I said.

"Rock-and-roll band," he said, as though correcting me.

"Rock. And we'll be practicing every Saturday afternoon."

"Saturday afternoon," he said, sounding like an echo chamber. He paused as though waiting for me to say more. When I didn't, he said: "What instrument do you play?"

"Drums."

"Didn't think it'd be the fiddle," he said. "In a rock-and-roll band." More silence. "But, then, you're not going to quit."

"Well, yeah," I said. "I'm gonna play drums." I thought maybe he didn't hear me.

"You're not quitting," he said. "You are just changing instruments."

I tried not to roll my eyes so he could see. "Well, yeah, I guess."

He put down his fiddle and picked mine from its case.

I felt bad. But Grandpa Gord had been teaching me old-time fiddle music. It's music of the old folk. Kids at school laugh at it.

I had never taken drum lessons or anything. But being around Grandpa Gord and taking music lessons had helped. I had often played around with the drums at Grandpa Gord's house. He always had a drum set in his basement so his own band could practice. The set belonged to one guy who no longer played with Grandpa Gord's band.

"You won't need this, then," he said, placing my fiddle carefully back in the case. "Just make sure you store it right so it doesn't get ruined. Take it out and play it once in a while so it stays in tune. If a fiddle doesn't get played, it gets rusty." He made the kind of grunty sound older people make when they try to stretch too far.

"So this band, it's — what? — like a garage band?" he asked again.

"Kinda."

"You been practicing?"

I tried to figure out what he was getting at. Sometimes with grandparents you have to know why they want to know something before you answer a question. It's tricky.

"Why?"

"Just interested, that's all. A band has to practice. Alone and together."

"Hockey, too."

"Anything you want to be good at, you have to practice. Work on your weak spots."

"Sure."

"Who's going to make sure you practice?"

I shrugged. "We just will. Every Saturday. Before or after hockey games. We will."

"Be sure you do. That's why most bands fail, eventually. They need someone to make sure they practice. Make sure they stay together."

"Like a manager."

"Yes, a manager can handle the non-musical stuff. But also a band needs somebody who can act as a coach. Don't make a face. A music coach is important."

"Yeah, I know," I said, but I had no idea what he meant. A hockey coach, yes. But for a band? "But we're together on this. We'll work it out."

"Be sure you give it your best."

"We will," I said. "We do. We really do."

"So? Have you practiced?"

Actually, we had been practicing at Ryan and Dylan's house. They're brothers. They're both on my hockey team. Ryan's in my class at school; Dylan's a year behind. They both had guitars. I had drumsticks and used an old practice pad that their father had left before he divorced their mother.

"Yeah."

"Good. What do you play?"

"Dunno. Rock, mainly."

"You said that. What kind?"

"AC/DC, Led Zeppelin, Def Leppard, Strange

Alliance. Stuff like that."

"That stuff's been around for a few years. You kids like that?"

I shrugged. "I do. Now they do. Dad gave me a bunch of his old tapes. He took me to an AC/DC concert at the Hangar last year."

"At the airport?" he asked.

Sometimes he surprised me. "The Air Canada Centre. We call it the Hangar."

"Oh."

"Because it's so ..."

"Your dad used to want to play the drums," he said.

What? This was news to me.

"But he didn't have drums to play on," he added. "That was after he married your mother. When you came along, they were lucky to afford a crib."

"I don't have drums yet, either," I confessed.

"Those bands you like," he added. "Lots of drum lines in those, if I remember."

"Yeah."

"Hard to practice without drums," he said. "But I guess you'll figure it all out. To me, this rock-and-roll still sounds like pots and pans, but my ears are different. Let me know when you're ready to get back to real music again."

With that, he closed the case with my violin in it, snapping the fasteners sharply as though they were closed forever.

5 Replacement Coach

Thursday night in the dressing room, twenty minutes before game time, somebody asked who was making out the player roster.

"Coach will do it when he gets here," said Simon Lee.

"He's late," someone observed.

"Be nice to win one for the coach, his last game," said Morley. Morley always looked for corny stuff: wins for the coach, cards for every girl in class on Valentine's Day, flowers for his mother on Mother's Day, a Stanley Cup for the Leafs. I used to believe in tooth fairies, too.

"Has anybody seen the coach yet?"

Everybody looked around at everybody else as though one of us was going to turn into Coach Rajah. When that didn't happen, some heads started shaking.

That's when Mr. Reisberry came into the dressing room.

"Where's Rajah?" he asked, his eyes darting

around the room.

"Not here yet," said Willie.

"Maybe he got lost," someone said. "The website said the arena was on Pebblestone Road."

Everybody laughed.

Most of our games were here at the South Courtice Arena on Prestonvale Road. Last year, some teams at the Backler Tournament ended up missing their first games because somebody had told them the rink was on Pebblestone Road. It was a pretty dumb mistake.

Mr. Reisberry turned on his heel and left. Two minutes later he was back.

"Rajah can't make it," he said. "He's stuck in traffic."

All the players' heads came up at once.

"No coach?"

"I can't," said Mr. Reisberry, as though that were a choice. "I just came to drop off Jamie. I have to pick up his sister from her game in Orono."

"We certainly need somebody behind the bench," said one of the parents.

Mr. Reisberry pulled out his cell phone as though that would fix everything. But before he could punch one button, before he had even decided who he would call, the dressing-room door burst open and crashed against the stick rack behind it.

P.J. jostled Mr. Reisberry off balance as he took two huge strides into the room. He tossed my helmet, face guard, and mouth-piece to me across the room.

"Here," he said. "You forgot your head. I told you it would happen one day."

Every head in the room came up.

Slowly, Mr. Reisberry turned to him and smiled.

"If you're not tied up for the next hour," he said, putting one arm around Grandpa P.J.'s shoulders, "we might have a job for you. Just for one game, of course."

"You mean now?" P.J. asked, looking at his watch.

"Well," said Mr. Reisberry, "the game is tonight."

P.J. gave a kind of smirk. He winked at Willie and me.

"What sort of job did you have in mind?" he asked.

Mr. Reisberry didn't even seem to notice that P.J. was pulling his chain.

"Coaching on the bench tonight," he said. "With Rajah not here, somebody has to do it. It's not really hard. All you have to do is open the door for the line changes. The kids know when to go on."

P.J. looked at him, a puzzled crease in his forehead.

"Oh, is that's all coaching is?" he said. "Then anybody could do it."

Mr. Reisberry kept smiling, "Then you'll do it?"

P.J. shook his head, smiled, shrugged, and said, "Sure, why not?"

Before the game, P.J. gathered the team around him at the bench.

"Same game plan as last game," he said. "Score goals.

Protect Jake. Don't let them get a second chance. Skate hard. Keep your stick on the ice."

Jamie looked at him. "Do you have any real advice we can use?"

P.J. blinked. "Okay, mister," he said. "Your line is now our fourth line." He pointed to the bench. "That real enough for you?" He pointed to Ryan. "Cutherbertson, your line starts." He looked at the sheet of paper in his hand, pointed toward Joseph Peleg and Frank Kennedy, then made a little sideways waving motion as though he were erasing something.

"Simon Lee, Richard," he said. "You're starting defence."

"But we already were starting defence," said Richard.

"Well, then, you have no problems, right?"

I headed for my goal to wait for the opening face-off. This was not going to be a fun game, that's for sure. P.J. was actually trying to coach.

The ref tooted his whistle. The players lined up. The game was on.

One thing P.J. may have missed — our starting line of Bill Routley, Carl Biro, and Jamie Reisberry was to match our best line against the opposing team's best line. To put Ryan on centre against the OPG Power Plugs' best line wasn't a good idea. But I wasn't going to say so.

I skated to my net, clinked the goalposts with my

stick, and waited for the game to start.

Right from the face-off, the OPG centre chipped the puck between Ryan's feet and stepped around him. With two strides he was at our blue line, moving fast. He had caught our defence standing still.

With two more strides, one to the left and one to the right, he rocketed between Simon and Richard. He not only split them — they collided behind him. He crossed the blue line. Halfway to goal, he cocked his stick back and slapped a shot at me.

I waved my glove hand at it. I felt it in the webbing. It was a hard shot that pulled my hand back and up before I lost sight of it.

My players around me yelled, but I couldn't hear them. Time seemed frozen.

P.J. had drilled it into me: if you don't know where the puck is, cover up.

I pulled my glove hand to my midsection to freeze the play. Instead of a whistle, I heard a huge groan from my players and the bench.

Immediately, I dropped flat in front of the goal line.

I could feel the puck under my ribs. I tried pulling it under me with my elbows.

One Power Plug, or maybe six of them, jabbed again and again at my side.

I wished Jamie had been on the ice that shift.

I felt a stab of pain as a stick found a soft spot under my pads. Then the ref whistled long and hard. I looked up to see him pointing straight down into the net.

The other team cheered.

I looked down in time to see that the puck was just over the line inside the goal.

1–0.

★★★

By the end of the first period the other team led us 4–0.

At the buzzer I skated to the bench.

"Drink," I said to P.J.'s blank stare. "There." I pointed to my water bottle with my blocker.

P.J. fussed a bit. "Keep your stick on the ice," he said. "Watch the five-hole."

I rolled my eyes.

"It's defence I need," I said. "Don't mix the guys up."

"Am I coach, or am I coach?" P.J. asked. "And the coach has to do what he can with the talent he has on the bench."

I handed back the bottle. "Just open the gate," I said quietly so the others couldn't hear me. "Don't embarrass me."

As I skated back to the goal at the far end I could hear him clearly. "We're doing okay. Just a little pep is all you need. Keep your heads up, your sticks on the ice. After a couple of practices, I'll have you guys in fine shape."

Yeah, right.

We ended up losing the game 9–3.

In the dressing room after the game, nobody spoke to me. Nobody spoke much at all.

I looked around the room. The MP3 players had come out and earphones were in. Some guys did a little humming or finger drumming to the music.

I knew a retreat when I saw one. Even Willie wouldn't look me in the eyes. And only half of the goals I let in were really my fault.

6 Punishing Practice

Since June, I had been letting my hair grow. It's kind of curly, and comes down over my ears. It's a rockin' look. Sometimes it hangs down over my eyes a bit, but I can see okay. All I have to do is shake my head.

First practice, that is what Grandpa P.J. pointed out. Rajah was really gone, and nobody else had come forward. For one more practice, P.J. would coach.

In the dressing room, just as I was about to put on my mouthpiece, helmet, and face guard, P.J. pointed at me from across the room.

"And you," he said, his finger drilling a hole in my forehead, "get a hair cut."

"I can see okay," I said weakly.

"And I'm Terry Sawchuk," he said.

Everybody but me stood and headed for the door.

"Who is Terry Sawchuk?" asked Willie, but even I knew he was kidding.

"The rest of you," P.J. said to the departing backs of

the players. "We're going to work hard out there today."

If anybody heard him, I didn't see any sign of it.

For a goalie, practices are harder work than a game. Unless your team really sucks and the other team is shooting at you all the time, you get some time to rest during a game.

In a practice, you don't. From the time we get on the ice until the time we come off — that's usually fifty minutes from Zamboni to Zamboni — they're all peppering shots at me. When I come off the ice, I look like someone has dumped a bucket of water over me, and I don't smell too good.

I wriggled my helmet on. On the way out of the dressing room I grabbed my stick from the rack. P.J. was ahead of me, just ready to step on the ice.

"You gonna lock the dressing room?" I asked, because I knew he hadn't. I was the last out of the room.

"Right."

He turned back to the dressing room, fishing for his keys.

I headed for the ice.

Once I got in the goal, I didn't even have time to scrape the ice on the crease, side to side. Before I even turned around, someone rang one off the crossbar.

They started shooting from all angles: from the point, from the other point, from the face-off circle, some in shoot-out style, some skating from centre ice. Some tried a wrap-around when they circled the net to get back their puck.

Coach Rajah had pretty well controlled this free-for-all. First, he didn't dump all the pucks on the ice at once. And he made sure he was first on the ice and got the team focused.

By the time Grandpa P.J. made it to the ice, I felt as though I was in a war zone.

"Hey!" said Grandpa P.J. as he opened the gate to come on the ice.

That anybody heard him was a miracle, but he does have a big voice. Everybody turned to see the new coach make his entrance.

P.J. stepped onto the ice. He turned around to close the gate behind him.

He slipped.

He flailed his arms to catch his balance. They churned like windmills. Then he added his legs to the dance. All I could see were arms and legs churning like a cartoon character falling form a cliff. P.J. slowly sank lower and lower, and then dropped with a thud to the ice.

The fall brought laughter from the team, followed by a round of stick-slapping applause as he tried to get to his feet.

P.J. is usually a good skater. Instead of applauding, I worried about the sound of that thud. From the look on his face, it had at least knocked his breath out of him.

"Bet you can't do that again!" someone yelled.

Several players laughed. Someone said, "This practice, we'll teach P.J. how to skate!"

P.J. rolled once and lifted himself on his knees. Using his stick, he pulled himself up.

"Grand entrance," he said, brushing off his knees. "Trick knee."

He produced a whistle and blew a long, shrill blast. With his arms he made a "gather-round" motion.

"Pucks in the net," he said, pointing with this stick to the empty net at the far end of the ice.

He signalled me to centre ice with the team.

"Okay, around the ice," he said. He pointed to Willie, who was the team captain.

"Willie, you lead. Single file. Four laps. Now."

Coach Rajah had never done this before.

"Like, skate around?" asked Willie. "Like, public skating."

P.J. rolled his eyes and brought his eyebrows together. "It's a warm-up, guys," he said. "Don't argue. Just do it. Pretend I'm Punch Imlach."

He looked at a circle of blank faces.

"Who's he?" asked Jamie.

"He used to … oh, never mind. Google it when you get home. Just skate." And he held his hockey stick out straight to his right. "Willie, now."

Willie started out slowly. The others followed. As the last player joined the little parade, P.J. touched me on the arm.

"You, too."

"Me? But I'm … "

"Yes, I know. A goalie. So am I. And goalies have to skate, too."

With a sigh, I followed.

Coach Rajah assumed everybody could skate. He spent the practice time on important stuff. He taught us position. He ran drills so everybody knew where to be when the puck was in our end, where to be when the puck was in the other team's zone. He didn't waste time on skating.

We diddled around for two laps. I passed a couple of guys, even with all my pads on.

After the third lap, P.J. blasted the whistle and made clockwise motions with his left hand. Since he was holding that stick in that hand, it was kind of a neat trick.

"Other way 'round," he said. "Other way. Simon, turn around."

Some stopped, sending ice chips into the air. Some, like me, just circled and came around the net and out the other side.

Three more laps we skated.

Another blast on the whistle.

"Backward!"

Some of the players looked at P.J. as though he had asked them to wear a dress.

"But I'm a forward!" protested Willie.

"And last year you ended up playing point on a power play," said P.J. "And who knows? This year you may have some shifts on defence. Maybe we shift everybody around. So get skating."

Willie didn't look pleased. One thing he does not do is skate backward. I'm a bit better at it, because I had played defence as well as goal. And a goalie often has to at least drift backward toward the goal to keep an eye on the puck.

Backward, we did the same thing: four laps. Then the whistle. Reverse direction.

We gathered at the bench.

"Weaknesses," P.J. said.

"Huh?"

"Weaknesses. That's what we're going to work on in practice. I want to know what is the weakest skill you have. The thing you do least best. And we'll work on it."

"But I ..." someone began.

"Uh-uh-uh," said P.J. waggling a finger. "Rule one: do what the coach says."

"Pick out your weakness. When I blow the whistle, you will have five minutes to work on that weakness. Five. Okay? Think, then go!" He tooted the whistle.

Slowly I skated back to the goal. Surely someone would say their weakness was not scoring goals, and want to practice. P.J. glided over to me.

"Your weakness?" he said.

"I dunno. I thought ..."

"Your weakness?"

I shrugged. I hadn't thought of that before.

"Then I'll tell you," said P.J. "Getting up. You get up slow, like you're rolling over from a nap. So here's the drill. Drop down on one knee, then get back up, then down on the other knee. That's it. Down. Up. Down. Up."

I repeated this a couple of times.

"Keep going," said P.J. "Only four minutes left."

While I repeated the drill a few more times. P.J. drifted from player to player. Some were shooting the puck against the boards. Some skated backward. Some got a puck and stick-handled around slowly.

After twelve times down and eleven times up, my legs wobbled. Sweat ran off my forehead. I struggled to get to my feet. P.J. skated around, talking to players one at a time. He made notes on the clipboard he had picked up from the bench.

Soon players went back to doing what they liked to do. Most liked to shoot the puck, if not at a goalie then at the boards. For some reason, Willie decided to take a slapshot from the point. It sure wasn't his weakness.

About the same time Jamie Reisberry decided to play Gretzky behind the net. This was about as silly as Willie practicing his slapshot. Reisberry stick-handled well. The only weakness I could see was his being self-ish and lazy. He hadn't learned to trust his teammates with a pass, and was good enough that he didn't need to. How do you practice that?

But there he was, behind the net, dipsy-doodling like the Great One himself: back and forth, back and forth, feigned wraparound.

That's when I saw Willie wind up.

I saw Willie's shot coming in — well, a little bit of it — and I thought maybe I should have tried to stop it. But it was off the goal by the width of my stick blade. It came through about the same time that Jamie wheeled around to face the boards behind the net.

Jamie caught the puck behind the knee. He went down like someone had clubbed him. He lay there, moaning, holding his leg right in that soft spot that has no padding.

I've felt Willie's slapshots *with* padding. I could imagine how he felt.

He tossed from side to side, squeezing behind his knee.

"Jeez, Willie," he said when he had stopped grimacing. "That hurt."

"Sorry," Willie said. "I didn't think ..."

P.J. looked down at Jamie, then at Willie. "That slapshot your weakness?" he said to Willie.

Willie looked at his laces. "Sorry," he said again.

Jamie got to his feet slowly. He skated over to the

bench, lifting his left leg up behind his knee repeatedly.

"Just let me skate this off," he said. "No big deal."

P.J. tooted his whistle "Okay, enough standing around. Everybody back to the goal line."

He looked at me. "You, too, Jake."

P.J. puffed out his chest like a parading pigeon. "Hockey is a skating game. So we need to practice skating. Here's what we will do. I blow this whistle, you skate to the far end. Rest. I blow the whistle again, you skate back here."

"But Rajah said we were going to work on positional play," said Jamie. "He said if we're in the right place, we don't need to skate as hard."

P.J. blinked under his helmet.

"But you have to skate hard to get in position," he said. "Last game, you lost the back-checking race thirty-one times. Thirty-one times — that's once a minute. Half of those were in the third period."

"But we just did seven laps!" said Dylan.

"Seven laps of warm-up," said P.J., "is not skating drill. Get ready!"

Toot. The whistle blew. We all started off, even me. I lumbered along.

At the far end, everyone stood waiting for me. P.J. skated up.

"Have a nice skate, boys?"

We all exchanged looks. A couple of the players glared at me.

"We're going to do that again. Only this time I want you all to skate hard, as fast as you can. No dogging it."

Toot. The team took off again.

I'll tell you one thing — skating lengths in full goalie gear is no fun. And another thing — it is useless. When is a goalie ever supposed to skate like that?

Again we huddled at the rink's end. I was sucking air. Even Dylan was puffing a bit. Willie, too.

"Better," said P.J.

Toot. Everybody stood, shocked for a second.

Then Dylan started off. Everybody followed. Even me.

This time I passed Jamie at the blue line and beat him in. I told you he wasn't that fast. Either that or he was dogging it.

"Good, good," said P.J.

"This time I want — "

"Not that old blue-line-to-blue-line drill," said Maurice Lambert. "That sucks."

"Mind your language, young fellow," said P.J.

"But I just said — "

"It's not what you said," said P.J. with a smirk. "It's that you said it. The Rocket here has it right: the same drill, end to end, except that you go to the far blue line, back to the first blue line, and then back to the far end."

"Like a race?" asked Dylan. Dylan was the smallest player on the team. He was fast but didn't like to be hit.

"Like a race," said P.J. "Just like every time you go for the puck in a game. It's a game of skating races."

Toot. We were off again. This time it was Dylan who led. Jamie turned at the second blue line just behind him. They turned to face me coming back. I could see Jamie was hurting. By the time I turned at the far blue line, some of the others had turned again. Several had passed Jamie.

At the far end, behind the goal line, several players collapsed into heaps.

P.J. had that annoying smile on his face. "Okay, you guys warmed up yet?"

"Warmed up?" said Jamie, a whine in his voice. "This is crap."

"Jamie, you have much more speed than you are using," P.J. said.

I glanced up to see Jamie's reaction. He shrugged.

"You do a good job of protecting your goalie," P.J. said. "But you are getting a rep in the league for mean hits."

Jamie looked up with pride.

"Use your skates more and your body less," P.J. said, "or you'll be on the bench."

P.J. turned back to the rest of the team, lined up on the far goal line.

"All set?" he said. "Check how you're holding your stick." I could see everybody on the team — and I mean everybody — look first at their hands and then back and forth at their teammates. Jamie shrugged.

They had no idea what he was talking about.

P.J. skated from player to player. "Number one: Two hands on the stick. Ever heard that before? When you can do ten reps, curling your own body weight with one hand," he said, "then you can use one hand."

A pause.

"Number two: keep your stick on the ice."

Another pause.

"Yeah, yeah, I know. It's a cliché. But things don't get to be clichés unless they are important. Number three: keep your lower hand down on the shaft of the stick. You, World Wide Willie, down on the shaft. Right."

He glided along in front of the team.

"Joseph, you, too. Down on the stick. No, don't hold it like it will break. What do you think it is, a violin? Hold it like you mean to break it if you have to. No one ever show you this before?"

Actually, nobody had. Maybe because it was dumb. I shrugged apologetically at my teammates, but I'm not sure if anyone was watching.

"Leverage," P.J. said. "With one hand on the stick, you have no power at all. With two hands close together you have not much more. Spread your hands. That's it. Like this."

Then he did what he should not have done.

He poked a puck ahead of him on the ice, gripped

his stick with his left hand two-thirds down the stick, leaned forward, and let a wrist shot go at the side boards.

Or he tried to, anyway.

When he leaned into it, putting all his weight on his left leg, his knee buckled.

The puck flipped in the air. It hit the boards with a small clunking sound, then wobbled to a stop. Grandpa P.J. struggled to regain his balance.

"Like that, Coach?" said Carl Biro. "Or are we supposed to stay on our feet?"

The team laughed.

That's what hurt me most, I think. The team laughed.

In the dressing room after the practice, Jamie threw his stick on the floor in disgust. I saw him talking in half whispers with his father. Mr. Reisberry kept looking at P.J. and nodding as his son talked.

Later, when we were getting drinks from the vending machine, I overheard Mr. Reisberry with Grandpa P.J.

"We need a coach who can keep these kids in line," Mr. Reisberry said. "That was pretty wild out there. Jamie could have been hurt, bad."

"It's discipline," said P.J. "Change of the guard and all that. They'll come around."

"And punishment drills went out of style years ago," Mr. Reisberry added. "But don't worry. When we find the right coach, this team will come around just fine."

He left then, hoisting Jamie's equipment over his shoulder. I glanced over at P.J. His eyes were distant and he didn't seem to have anything to say.

7 Tree Trimming

Sunday at our house that week was, for me, a skunky day. My parents and grandparents were laughing and singing and having a good time. It was Grandpa Gord's birthday. He was sixty-eight, which is pretty old.

But I could tell he was not happy.

First of all, his birthday party was combined with our Christmas tree hunt.

Every year, Mom and Fred hold this Christmas tree party. Mom invites everybody: my dad, Grandpa Ron, Grandpa Gord and Nanny Joyce, P.J., and bunches of cousins, mostly girls, who giggle and drive me crazy. This year even my Uncle Roly came with his six daughters. The house was full.

The idea of the party is to get all bundled up like animated penguins and go marching across the frozen snow to find a Christmas tree. Then Fred cuts it down. We carry it home and tie it up like a prisoner in the living room. My cousins — the girls, anyway — all decorate it, and Mom and Nanny Joyce spend the rest of the day rearranging the decorations because the little kids put everything on the lower branches and nobody puts anything behind the tree.

All day P.J. went on and on about the team to anyone who would listen and to several who didn't. I didn't talk to him once. He was talking as though he was the coach, while Jamie's Reisberry's father was out doing his best to find somebody else.

Things with my Grandpa Gord were awkward. I knew he felt bad about my not playing the fiddle any more, so I didn't talk to him either. I just stuffed my earphones into both ears and cranked up the volume on my MP3 player.

The whole tree thing got to me, too. Imagine plodding across the fields of a Christmas tree farm to track down a tree, and then killing it by cutting it off at the roots, and dragging it home to display in the living room. When I was a kid it used to make me happy. Today it didn't.

What if trees went out to hunt down people, wrapped them up in baler twine, and carted them back to the tree farm so they could stand them in the middle of the field and string lights on them? How would you like to be a Christmas human for happy trees?

That's what I said to Grandpa Ron. He didn't understand what I was getting at.

"There is nothing wrong with harvesting Christmas

trees," he said, as though it was something I wanted to debate. "It takes seven years to grow a tree, that's all. It doesn't degrade the environment. Christmas trees are a renewable resource. They're a crop, just like corn or wheat or turnips."

I never did like turnips.

When I didn't respond, and didn't even smile, he waited until others had gone on to other things. Then he ushered me into the den.

"Sorry your dad couldn't make it today," he said.

"Yeah."

My dad hadn't made it to one of my games this year. It was a three-hour drive each way from London, but Grandpa Ron lives there, too, and he made it to a lot of them.

"I've told him he should get his schedule in order so he can get down here more often."

I was supposed to see my dad every second weekend. Lately, that hadn't happened. But it wasn't Grandpa Ron's fault, so I didn't say anything.

"So what's the problem?" Grandpa Ron asked.

"Huh?"

"Help if you took out your ear plugs."

"Huh?" I repeated, shaking my hair away from my ear so I could take out one earphone. "Couldn't hear. Had my player on."

"Kids," he said. Just that one word, the way only a grandparent could say it. Then he added; "You're going to ruin your ears."

I grinned, turned off my player, shook my hair loose and took out the other earphone.

"That's what Dad said you used to say about him when he was my age listenin' to rock."

Grandpa Ron smiled a thin smile. "You ever try to talk to your dad? You think he just doesn't listen. That's not it. He can't hear. So I rest my case."

He was kidding, I think.

Grandpa Ron dropped into the one big stuffed chair in the den. He pulled one leg up to rest on the knee of the other leg, showing off socks that did not match.

"So what *is* the problem?" he said.

"Nothing"

"You haven't talked to anyone all day. Are you becoming a recalcitrant teen?"

"Don't even know what that is."

"Neither do I, but it sounds important."

Some of my girl cousins danced and shrieked in the TV room.

Grandpa Ron said, "P.J.'s coaching your team, I hear."

How could he help but hear? P.J. had been broadcasting it all day.

"I guess. Until they find a real coach."

"P.J. seems to think it's pretty well a done deal."

"Hunm."

"He's planning a lot of stuff for you guys."

I looked at Grandpa Ron. I shrugged.

Grandpa Ron smiled.

"He made some changes in his own life so he could coach your team. It's something that doesn't happen often. You should enjoy it, appreciate it."

"Yeah, right," I said.

A loud blast of laughter came down from upstairs.

"Look," he said. "You've been lucky enough these past three years to have a coach like Raj who really, really knows hockey. He played Major Junior, has a couple of gold rings, knows a lot of big names in the game. So you've been lucky. Usually guys like that coach rep or triple-A."

I examined my feet.

"I've told you many times I went to school with Bobby Hull. That doesn't make me an expert. But I do know some stuff about the game. And your grandpa P.J., he knows even more. He still plays hockey, for goodness' sake."

I knew he would bring up that thing about Bobby Hull. Even Hull's son, Brett, is retired. Nobody I know even knows who he is, except Simon Lee, who spends all his time on the Internet looking at hockey stats.

"Sometimes you guys do too much," I said.

Grandpa Ron looked at me strangely.

He was perhaps the most normal of my grandfathers. Except for the mismatched socks.

"And what's this thing about your rock band?" he asked. "Serious?"

"Yeah."

"And Gord says you're not playing the fiddle any more."

"Yeah."

"For good?"

"No, for drums. Can't play a fiddle in a rock band."

Sometimes adults can be as dumb as a bass drum.

"Ah, rock!" But he said it like rock wasn't real music. He said it like Grandpa Gord said it.

"Just don't spurn Gord," he said. "He really enjoyed teaching you the fiddle."

"What do you mean?"

"Sometimes we have to put some effort into staying close to the people we love. I keep telling that to your dad, too."

"Yeah," I said, but I wasn't sure what he was getting at.

We both sat there in the den, not speaking. Finally, I said, "I need drums."

Grandpa Ron tried a weak smile that looked more like grimace. "So your dad said. You got it on your Christmas list? Does Santa know?"

"Santa's already told me that drums cost too much."

"He couldn't get them down the chimney anyway. So what are you going to do?"

"Dunno. Steal hub caps, or wheels off baby buggies."

"Oh, I see."

Just then Grandpa Gord opened the den door.

"They're about ready to serve dinner," he said. He looked at me for a moment without speaking. He held on to the den door, kind of leaning into the room.

"Want to play some tunes later?" he asked.

"Tunes?" I asked.

"Yes," said Grandpa Gord. "Like we usually do. Fiddle tunes."

I shrugged. "No. Not today."

But what I was thinking was, *not ever.* Why couldn't he just get that message?

Grandpa Ron gave me a strange look.

★ ★ ★

As usual my mother had prepared a tree-hunting cake. She does that every year. Not that she makes it herself: it's a fancy cake with trees make of icing and little plastic figures of lost children with sleighs. Usually the cake is good.

When Nanny Joyce came into the room, I asked her, "When are you coming to see me play?"

"Your band?" she said.

"No, my hockey team," I replied, laughing.

She made a sour face. "Get away with you," she replied. "I just couldn't bear to see you get hurt. You know that."

This year my mother and Nanny brought out a second cake, a surprise cake for Grandpa Gord. This one had a big fiddle in icing. Everyone sang "Happy Birthday" off key. Then they brought out a big present for him.

Well, not big like a car or a house. It was about a metre long and a third of a metre wide and half that deep.

Grandpa Gord looked from face to face. He didn't like getting presents. I knew that. He had that look that a bunny rabbit gets when you scare him out of the backyard garden — eyes frozen in panic, his legs poised to run.

Carefully, he removed the paper, the way older people do — afraid to rip the paper, so they could use it again. Of course, with any of my grandfathers that just might happen.

With the paper tugged off you could see it was a fiddle case.

"Open it, Dad," said my mother.

"It's from all of them," said Nanny Joyce. "All of the kids." My mother has a sister and two brothers, other than Uncle Roly. They live in the Maritimes and British Columbia and we don't see them often.

Grandpa Gord turned the case around on his knee. Without looking up, he said, "You shouldn't have."

The thing is, he meant it. Maybe I was the only

one who could hear that in his voice.

He clicked the release on the two catches and opened the case. Inside was a violin.

"It's special," said Mom and Fred together.

"For you," said Uncle Roly.

Grandpa Gord lifted the fiddle out of its case as though it was made of egg shells.

"You shouldn't have," he repeated, holding up the fiddle for everyone to see.

Later, when we did play some tunes, it was his old fiddle that he played.

8 No Show

Two things happened at our next game. Neither I want to remember.

First — Jamie didn't show up.

The second was why Jamie didn't show up. Remember that Jamie's dad was the sponsor of the team? He quit, too.

The night before, P.J. had phoned me, all excited. The league had made him coach to replace Rajah. What he didn't know when he showed up in the dressing room was what everybody else seemed to: the sponsor had pulled out.

"He what?" P.J. said, when Carl Biro told him that Jamie had quit.

"And his dad, too," Carl had added, adjusting his earphones.

"Jamie's dad does not play," said P.J., picking up a stick from the rack by the door. He held the stick upside down and thumped the butt on the floor.

Don't ask me why.

"But he's the sponsor," said Carl.

That's when one of those silences fell on the dressing room. If you've been in a dressing room, you know how noisy they can be. Everybody chatters. It's hard to hear.

This time, everybody stopped talking at the same time. Everybody looked up at P.J.

"So?" P.J. said finally.

"We need a sponsor, don't we?" asked Willie.

"Jamie said his dad was pissed off about that practice on Tuesday," said Dylan. "All that skating. And then Jamie getting hurt."

Several players nodded. "It was cruel," someone said.

"Jamie said he never had to skate like that playing triple-A," said Willie. "Said it didn't make sense."

"Besides, his father couldn't find another coach," said Joseph. "We're stuck with you, P.J." He said it kindly, as though it wasn't the worst thing in the world, and a few others laughed.

"Well, I was bagged when I got home," said Maurice. "Defence shouldn't have to skate so hard."

P.J. chuckled. "Tell that to your goalie. Goalies all want the defence to skate faster. And backward. And forwards should skate hard back-checking. Your job is to protect the goalie."

Joseph shrugged.

"Anyway," said P.J. holding up his hands. "Guys.

Guys, pay attention a minute."

The silence fell again. Not all the earphones came out.

"Look, I'm disappointed that Jamie isn't here. He has legs and can score if he wants to, and he does work hard at protecting his goalie. But he's not here tonight, so it just means that the rest of you are going to have to skate even harder. You don't have Jamie to take up the slack. So I don't want anybody hanging back tonight. You skate hard each shift. You do that, you can beat these guys."

These guys were the Moxley Movers. They were in first place, and hadn't lost a game. In those seven games they had given up only five goals. And they had three shutouts. Their goalie was hot.

"One more thing," P.J. continued. "The sponsor has already paid for your sweaters. So the sponsor thing is between me, the manager, the league officials. Your job is to ... hey, hey, hey, all attention here."

The eyes all focused back on P.J.

"Your job is to go out there and skate. Your job is to play hockey."

"Yeah, yeah," said Carl.

"It can't be any worse than the practice," said Frank Kennedy. "That was — "

But before he could finish the sentence, P.J. put his finger to his lips and made a shushing sound.

"Yes, it could be worse," said P.J., talking to Frank,

but loud enough for everyone to hear. "In a practice there is no scoreboard, and no public humiliation. Let's do it."

★ ★ ★

We tried. At least for a while.

Without Jamie, our defence could not hold them. When other guys are jabbing you in the ribs with sharp sticks and clubbing your hands with the heel of a blade, you kind of appreciate having someone with a mean streak on your side.

And with three forward lines and three sets of defence, P.J. had to juggle. I mean, Rajah would have juggled lines. I don't think P.J. knew what it meant to juggle lines, or change on the fly.

In the first period, Dylan and Ryan got double shifted. Now, I knew that Dylan could skate. But it seemed as though, when he moved to centre of the top line, he behaved like a centre for the top line.

So there we were in the first period. And these guys from Moxley dominated. That's my big word for the day: *Dom-in-8-ed*. Which means they kept the puck in our end most of the time.

A lot of the time they just walked in and blasted from six metres in front. When that happened, I just kicked out a pad and hoped. That's all you can do. You sure don't see much.

But somehow P.J.'s talk, or something, got through to our guys. Instead of hanging back, waiting for the other guys to do something like deke around them and shoot on goal, our guys started to go after them — even when they knew the other guy would get to the puck first. When they went after the other guys, a strange thing happened. Sure, the other team was still beating us to the puck. But with P.J. yelling and our guys skating, the other team just didn't have much time to do anything with the puck.

We were taking away their space.

It worked so well that we were only down 2–0 halfway through the period.

That's when the miracle happened.

One of their guys dug the puck out of the corner to my right. He threw a pass up along the boards to the point. I hunkered down, getting ready for the shot. I knew the opposing defence out there. With any time to prepare, he had a slapshot that came in head-high like a UFO.

Dylan headed from the top of the circle out to the point, challenging for the puck. Everybody in the rink knew the point defence would get the puck first. Still, Dylan skated like he knew he could beat the guy, rushing whatever time the guy might have had.

"Skate! Skate! Skate!" yelled P.J. from the bench.

Dylan did.

The other team's defence pulled the puck back and

began to cock his stick back for a slapshot. He saw that Dylan was too close. He changed his mind. Quickly, he wristed a shot.

The shot caught Dylan on the left shin and bounced outside the blue line. Dylan jabbed once at the puck and bounced it off the boards. He caught the defence flat-footed. Before he could turn, Dylan grabbed the loose puck and took off.

The opposite defence cut across ice, turned to coast backward. He crossed paths with Dylan just outside the other team's blue line.

Then Dylan did something I thought only pros could do. He deked to his left, jabbed the puck ahead between the defence's legs, skirted to the right, picked up the loose puck, and broke in on goal.

All alone.

The goalie stood his ground, riding out on the edge of the crease.

Dylan faked right, began to move left, then roofed it to the top right-hand corner. Crosby couldn't have done it better.

Our bench exploded. I slapped the ice with my goalie stick.

Maybe we wouldn't miss Jamie as much as I thought.

Dylan scored another, and Ryan got one. Carl, too.

In the third period, we were behind by only two, the score at 5–3. Then our wheels kind of fell off and they swarmed us.

Our guys had skated their best, but now their best was all gone. P.J. didn't say anything about stamina, but I am sure everybody remembered what he had said at practice.

The final score was 7–3, and we still needed a team sponsor. For better or worse, we had a coach.

9 Bad Test

Just when I thought things could not get any worse, they did.

First, at school I flunked a math test. Don't ask me how that happened. Usually I ace math. It's the one subject that I don't have to do homework in. I can solve the problems in my head. This test was on formulas or, as the teacher calls them, formulae. I think she must have spoken Latin as a kid.

So when I got home that afternoon, sure enough, the first thing my mother asked was: how was the math test. I pulled the crumpled test out of my back pack. She looked at it.

"Okay, mister. Lockdown rules."

"But Mom ..."

"No ifs, ands, or buts," she said. "Lockdown. No hockey, no band practice, no TV, no computer games until after your homework has been done."

I don't know how lockdown goes at your place, or

what you call it. Some, like Willie, get grounded and can't move. Others, like Victoria, never get grounded. But then Victoria always does her homework and not only scores almost perfect on every test, but gets the bonus marks as well. She does this even when she travels all over Ontario playing on the Clarington rep team. She gives the rest of us a bad name.

"But I have a hockey game tonight," I said, pleading. (Pleading is something like a whine with muscle.)

"If you have a hockey game tonight," she said, "then you better do your homework now."

"But ..."

"All of it. Now."

Long ago I learned that when my mother makes a rule, it stays enforced.

I did homework.

★ ★ ★

In the dressing room before the game that night, another surprise waited for me.
No Willie.

"I think he quit," somebody said. "Isn't everybody going to quit?"

Several heads nodded. That's when I knew the whole situation was bad. Worse, even, that I thought. Willie wouldn't quit. Would he?

When P.J. came back in the room, everybody shut up.

"Okay, guys," P.J. said, rubbing his hands together "This is a game for third place in the league. We're playing Orc Refrigeration and Cooling. These guys score a lot, but they give up a lot, too. Let's cool 'em"

"First of all," he continued "some news."

All the faces turned toward him.

"It seems that the league officials have looked everywhere, but they can't find a coach."

Several players groaned. "That sucks," somebody said.

"So rather than have no team," P.J. went on, "it looks as though you're stuck with me."

"As coach?" somebody asked.

"No, doofus, as left defence." He looked around the room. He didn't see a lot of happy faces. He started counting.

"Willie not here? Jamie, too." He pulled a piece of paper out of the hip pocket of his jeans. He scanned down it, peered up once, and looked like he was thinking.

"Hmm. We're going to be down to two lines. And you guys thought my skating drills in practice were tough."

The forwards would be on every other shift. That meant lots of ice time: in three ten-minute periods, fifteen shifts of one minute each. I didn't need a calculator to figure that out.

"You guys up to that?" P.J. asked, looking mainly

at the forwards.

Some, like Frank Kennedy, brightened. He always complained about not getting enough ice time. Even Coach Rajah was tired of Frank going on about it. He always said that if you dig in each shift you won't have enough energy to complain about ice time.

Others looked rebellious. P.J. paid no attention.

"Okey-dokey. Defence are all here. This means we might have to throw some defence onto a forward line. Mix things up. That's good. I wanted to start juggling, anyway."

With a stub of a pencil he made some marks on the paper. Even with the dressing room door closed, I could hear cowbells. Grandpa Gord had arrived to watch the game.

★ ★ ★

P.J. was right. The Orcs gave up goals easily. Right away, we jumped out to a 2–0 lead.

For a while I thought we stood a chance.

Late in the second period, while we were still up 5–2, our forwards began to slow down. Instead of skating back hard to back-check, they started to cruise, depending on the defence to stop the rush and on the goalie to stop the shots. The trouble is, without our forwards back-checking hard, the Orcs forwards had extra time with the rush. With no one on their heels, they could get fancy.

With five minutes to go in the second period, our defence started backing up with a three-on-two. Maurice was good, but with a three-on-two the other team has an extra man.

Their forward came right down the centre. Maurice lined him up, forcing him to go wide to my left. Maurice rode him right into the corner. But the centre dropped a pass at the top of the circle that his winger picked up. That left Joseph Peleg to face the winger with the puck, with another winger floating free. Joseph had to decide: does he let the guy with the puck shoot, relying on me, or does he go for the puck and let the guy pass to the other winger right out front?

From my goal crease I see those decisions all the time. This time Joseph hesitated just a fraction, leaving himself neither on the puck nor on the pass.

The winger faked a shot. I went left, high on the crease to cut his angle. Then he passed to his winger to my right.

I came over fast, but was too late. The guy had a tap in. I had no chance. Score was 5–3.

I think then they knew they had us.

Worse, P.J. started putting guys like Ryan and Dylan back on defence. That looked good, once, when Ryan picked up a pass off the face-off. Being back on defence gave him room to roam. He circled once, dipped around their right winger, deked the other team's left defence, and walked in on goal. There, he dragged the goalie out, made him commit, and then, with the whole open net to drop it into, he rang one off the goalpost so that it echoed all the way to me at the far end.

But the very next face-off, the Orcs came rushing at us. Dylan tried to turn and skate backward against the rush. He tripped. He slid along the ice on his back.

The forward did not wait to see if he was okay. With the whole wing open, he poured down on me, drifted into the face-off circle with loads of time, and blasted a slapper.

I kicked out one pad and caught the corner of it. But I was down, one leg stretched way out. I grabbed the puck in my glove, but their winger came in and tapped my glove. The puck dribbled out and over the goal line. 5–4.

We didn't do too well after that.

The third period: I don't want to talk about it. It is enough to say that they ended up beating us 11–6. Four of those goals came after I had made the initial save. The other team was all over my crease. Two of the goals came after I thought I had frozen the puck. But the ref didn't see it that way.

Maybe it was that Jamie wasn't there to help keep the Orcs out of the crease. But to tell the truth, it was not my best game. Even Grandpa Gord didn't ring the cowbells much. He didn't have much to ring them for.

In the dressing room afterward, everyone was down. Bill Glendinning threw off his shoulder pads in disgust. Nobody wanted to make much eye contact, especially with me.

Nobody said much. Even P.J. was quiet. After games he had taken to locking the dressing-room door for a five-minute talk with the team, just as Coach Rajah had done — without the parents. It was a good idea. Parents often complicate things.

This time, P.J.'s team time took less than a minute.

"Get everybody here, we'll beat them," P.J. said.

"Yeah," said Morley quietly.

P.J. shrugged. He walked to the door and unlocked it.

The parents milled in, also quiet. They shuffled around, shifting from foot to foot. Finally, Carl's father came over to me.

"He's going to be all right, you know," he said in a whispery kind of voice, as though he was afraid I would shatter.

"Who?" I asked, looking up from my seat on the bench.

"He doesn't know," someone else said. I felt the room go cold.

"Your grandpa."

I looked over at P.J. He looked all right to me.

"Not him. Grandpa Cowbells."

I shivered, suddenly scared.

"Right after the game, he collapsed. The ambulance just left. Your mother and Fred went with him."

All of a sudden I felt very alone.

10 Yesterday's Game

The next day, my mother and Fred were at the hospital all day. Nobody told me much, except that Grandpa Gord was very ill. But from the long faces and whispered voices, I knew that he was very, very ill.

When I returned from school there was nobody home. A few minutes later, Grandpa P.J. pulled up his van with the vanity plates — *P Pete J*. His name is really Peter James, and some people do call him Pete. But when you say P.J., everybody knows who you mean.

"Okay, you all ready?" he said as he came through the front door.

"Ready?" I asked.

"Yeah. We've got a few stops to make. First, we're going to stop at the hospital to see Gord. Then I've got some more stuff lined up. Where's your equipment?"

I was sure he did not mean band equipment. "Hockey equipment?" I asked, just to be sure.

"Is there any other kind?" he asked back, reaching over to tweak my nose as he used to do when I was seven. I ducked, as I have done since I was nine. "Yeah, bring it. I've got something special planned."

Maybe he has a practice planned, I thought. Strange as it seemed, I lugged my equipment up from the basement and took it out the van.

"Where do I put it?" I asked.

Grandpa P.J.'s goalie equipment took up all the cargo space in the back of his van.

"Throw it in the back seat," he said. "Or put the seats down. Whatever it takes."

So we drove off in a van filled with enough equipment for two hockey goalies.

"This is not the way to the hospital," I said as he turned left toward Bowmanville. "I'm sure they said he was in hospital in Oshawa."

"He is. But it's an hour before visiting hours and there's something I want to show you first."

I shrugged. You can tell when an adult is lying. This time I didn't fight it.

When we reached Bowmanville, P.J. pulled into the parking lot at the Rickard Arena.

"We gotta see a man about a horse," he said.

"I don't need a horse," I said.

"I want you to see something."

I followed him through the west doors. He veered to the right into the Clarington Hall of Fame, a display of sports figures from Clarington over the years. But P.J. didn't slow down for any of them.

"Here," he said, turning toward a sign that said *Brian McFarlane's Total Hockey*.

"Brian McFarlane is a famous hockey announcer," he said. I shrugged.

"I thought maybe you'd learn some of the history of the game here."

P.J. paid the cashier. I followed him through the door.

"It's a collection of a lot of stuff to show how hockey has developed," he said. "Maybe you can see where we come from. Where I come from."

We walked from exhibit to exhibit. At some, P.J. stopped and pointed.

He pointed to a pair of strap-on skates. "My father told me about learning to skate on those," he said. "I thought they were ancient."

In another glass case was a pair of Bauer skates with leather worn thin at the ankles. "Those were my skates when I was your age," P.J. said.

"You really wore skates like that?" I asked, pointing at the crackled leather uppers and tendon guards.

"Some kids even wore ankle supports because the boot was soft. It took a lot of skating to build ankle strength. If you wanted to play hockey, you had to work at it.

We moved on.

"There's my hockey game." On the wall hung two

old-fashioned table hockey games. One had metal players and push rods to make the players move and spin. The other had a rounded top at centre ice and bent wire, with painted red and white dowels for the players.

"Looks boring," I said.

"Here, pull this," he said. "No, not my finger, this," he said, pointing at a spring coil. "See? All the players move. The goalie just wags from side to side."

"That's it?"

"I was even younger than you are when we played that. I think I was nine when I bought mine with money from a farm job — $9.95 from the Eaton's catalogue. The Munro hockey game. We would get together and play tournaments. One kid in town, his mother had a kitchen range with a timer so we could play timed games."

"Huh." I wasn't really that impressed. But with Grandpa Gord being sick, somehow what P.J. said seemed more important.

There were three or four other displays. One was a stick-handling exercise. You had to move the puck from one marked circle to another as the lights came on. Another checked goalie reaction time. You had to slap circles on an upright board in front of you as they lit up.

"Can I try that?" I asked.

P.J. shrugged. "Go ahead. Although I have something even better for later."

I tried it. The game gave you thirty seconds to run through the lights. I scored forty-two.

Grandpa P.J. tried it. He scored thirty-eight.

"Ah, youth," he said. "Try this one." he said. The booth offered to clock the speed of a hockey shot.

I picked up a stick and tried one — thirty-seven miles an hour.

Considering that the pros can shoot a hundred miles an hour or more, I was humbled. But I'm a goalie.

"Try it again," P.J. said.

I wound up and got my best slapshot away — forty-five miles an hour.

"Better," P.J. said.

He pulled a stick from the rack and dribbled the puck back and forth. He let go a firm wrist shot that made a loud thud against the backboard.

The clock displayed his speed — 55.

"Gotta have some wrist to clear the puck," he said with a smirk. "But that's enough here. Let's go."

As we left, he said, "Some life left in the old guy yet," to no one in particular, looking back on the displays.

★ ★ ★

The hospital floor was quiet. The room Grandpa Gord was in looked down on the playground in the park across the street.

"He's resting," said my mom.

Grandpa Gord lay on the bed, firmly wrapped in the sheet. Two little plastic tubes ran into his nose. He breathed slowly. Tubes and wires were taped to his arms. A small screen showed a graph with his heartbeat.

"He was awake a while ago. The doctor says he's going to be fine, but what a scare."

Seeing Grandpa Gord asleep in a hospital bed made me feel empty.

P.J. looked at both Fred and Mom. "I'm taking Jake out for dinner and stuff," he said. "And I'll make sure he does his homework."

"You're sure it's no bother?" asked Mom.

P.J. looked at me. "Sure, Jake's always a bother. But what else is new?"

On the elevator to the main floor P.J. didn't say a word.

11 Old-timer Hockey

Grandpa P.J. drove north on Harmony to the Legends Sports Arena. It has four ice pads, a swimming pool, a fitness gym, and a library.

"What's this about?" I asked.

"You'll see. Bring your pads."

P.J. took such big steps, I could hardly keep up with him. Across the parking lot, he carried the goalie equipment as though it was light. I followed behind, balancing pads, stick, and equipment bag. I tried to match his big strides.

"Through here," he said, bulling his way through doors to the second ice pad to the left. He continued along and pushed open the dressing-room door.

"Hey, P.J.!" said a man half-dressed in his hockey equipment. "The Eagle can't make it tonight so we're just going to have a skate."

P.J. turned to me. "The Eagle is Eddie. He's the other goalie who plays in this Thursday night pickup game."

He turned back to the man as two, three others came through the door.

"Eddie called me yesterday and said he couldn't make it. But I brought along another goalie." He pointed at me.

The men looked at me. "Him?" the first man asked.

"My grandson. I didn't think I'd ever have a chance to play against him." He turned to me. "You up for that? You'll have to let some of these old guys score once in a while, otherwise their feelings will be hurt."

I shrugged. "I guess," I said.

Over the next few minutes the dressing room filled up with men of different ages, all acting just like my team did before a game.

One of the players cleared a place on the bench beside him and plunked down a boom box. He clicked it on and slid in a CD. AC/DC pumped out, filling the room even fuller.

I found a corner and started dressing.

"You like this stuff?" yelled the player with the CD player.

"What stuff?" I asked. "You mean hockey?"

"Naw. The music. You young guys likely have your own."

"AC/DC," I said. "One of my favourites. My band plays it."

"Good taste," he yelled over the music, showing me a thumbs-up.

Across the room, P.J. started dressing, too, and the room burst with pumping music, stale sweat, and men my dad's age teasing other men as though they were thirteen.

Strangely, I felt right at home.

Just before I slid my face mask in place, P.J. tapped me once on the pads.

"We have about fifty minutes," he said. "They'll divide up the skaters to keep things even. No ref. No hits. But watch it. There are no slapshots, but some of these guys can shoot hard."

He dropped his mask over his face and skated to the far end.

Gingerly, I stepped on the ice and glided to my own goal.

The warm-up was short. A few of the players skirted the blue line, circled in, and let shots go at me. One rang off the goal post. Then somebody blew a whistle.

All the pucks but one were rounded up into a bucket. One of the players from the other side held up the one remaining puck, dropped it to the ice, and circled behind P.J.'s goal.

The game was on.

The first rush got to my blue line. The forward overskated the puck. The action went back the other way.

Back and forth, end to end. These guys were old. Some looked pretty soft. But when they were on the ice, they hustled. I wished the Roofers could see this.

Then one of our players, the guy who did the most talking, started from behind my net, deked around three players at centre ice, went wide around the defence, circled the net at the far end, and beat P.J. to the far post to score on a wrap-around.

The teams returned to their original positions. One player from the other team dug the puck out of the net and started up the ice again.

This time he broke around our defence. He rushed in on me, full speed. I glided to the edge of the crease and held my ground. He tried a deke but I slid across with him, the way P.J. had taught me, and the puck dribbled off into the corner.

"Ohhhhhh!" said all four players on our bench.

"Way to go, Jake!" someone yelled.

A couple of plays later, one of their defence let one go from the blue line. It was a wrist shot, high and to my left. I jabbed at it with my blocker. Even through the padding I could feel the puck.

"Great stop, Jake!"

After I had made those first three or four stops, the players seemed to settle down. The play rushed up and down the ice. All the forwards either didn't have the legs for back-checking or they trusted the defence and goalie a lot.

Ten minutes into the game, one of their forwards, the guy with the boom box in the dressing room circled in front of P.J. He took two quick hops with blades flashing and caught our forwards going the wrong way. Just over centre, he made one small move against two of my defence. He dipped around them and was clear. He came in on a breakaway.

I hunkered down, trying to read him. But he was bigger and faster than anyone I've ever played against before. From the blue line he lined up a wrist shot.

One guy in my regular league has a slapshot timed at 70 miles an hour. I've stopped him.

But this guy, with just a wrist shot, beat me cleanly.

It went in the net over my right shoulder. I didn't have time to move.

Our captain skated over to pull the puck out of the net.

"Don't worry about that, kid," he said. "Loney's an old pro."

"I didn't even see it," I said.

"Thirty years ago he played in the old American Hockey League. Even moved up for a few games in the big league."

"Pro?" I said.

"He's beaten a lot of goalies."

I nodded. These were some of the guys P.J. faced every week.

To get even, the captain started out his rush slowly,

but hit the far blue line at top speed. This time he circled the net behind P.J., drifted backward into the face-off circle, and let a hard, low shot go.

P.J. got one pad on it. Even from my end, I could hear the thunk.

But P.J. had drifted forward out of his crease and went down with one leg almost straight out.

He rolled to get back on his feet. He struggled. I thought about the drill he put me through: up, down, up, down.

The puck bounced out to the blue line. The defence passed it to the left winger, who looped the puck high into the open net. P.J. was still struggling to get up on his knees.

When he did get to his feet, he looked at me across the length of the rink. He lifted both arms with a shoulder shrug. It said, *What can you do?*

The rushes came faster.

Having seen me stop a few good shots, the opposing players stopped treating me like I was made of glass. The shots came like they meant it.

The old pro, Loney, came in a second time.

He made almost the same moves as before: he caught the forwards napping, deked the defence out of their jockstraps, and came in on me like it was a shootout.

This time I was high in the crease. If he was going to shoot from out there, I would give make myself a big target. Even if I didn't see the shot, I thought he'd be more likely to hit me than an open spot in the net.

I was wrong.

This time he came in even further. In a fraction of a second, he was too close to shoot. I started to follow him to the left as he began a deke.

That's when he shot.

At least, I think that's what he did. His wrist shot was low, hard, and quick. Somehow I got a pad on it. I felt it go *thump*. My leg hurt.

But now I was down. The rebound spun out in front of the net, between the two face-off circles. Loney stopped, grabbed the puck, and gave it a nonchalant flip into what to him was an open net.

I dove for it. My stick came across and caught the puck, batting it out of the crease and into the corner.

From our bench came yelps of cheers. Sticks slapped on the boards.

The pro followed the puck into the corner, and then he just stood there. Even from the opposition bench I could hear cheers.

Then all the players on the ice slapped their sticks on the ice. Even P.J. at the far end slapped, and slapped, and slapped.

Loney drifted closer to the net behind the goal line. Finally, he let a pass go that our team intercepted to begin a rush to the far end.

Loney didn't bother to follow. He drifted toward my crease.

"Great stop, kid," he said, tapping me lightly on the pads. "You got the moves."

★ ★ ★

After the game, P.J. waved me down to his end of the ice. Somebody appeared with a camera. We had our picture taken together in our goalie equipment.

Later, in the dressing room, Loney cranked up the CD player.

One of the players said to P.J. "Hey, Grandpa, You should bring your grandson every week to give us some challenge."

"I thought you were having a nap a few times out there," said another to P.J. Over the music, he shouted to me, "Once P.J. goes down, he's like a Ninja Turtle with a backpack."

Amid the noisy, after-game gabble, Loney turned to me. He had grey hair and blue eyes like steel. "You should have seen P.J. even ten years ago," he said, as though in confidence. "He still had half the moves of his youth."

Everybody laughed.

"If P.J. had the chance at your age, he could have been pro," he said. I looked at him, searching for a smirk. But he meant it.

"Heck, he still knows the game better than a lot of guys who did make it. Let me tell you, I've had some coaches ..."

P.J. turned up the CD player. More ancient rock poured out.

Music. Hockey. Sometimes age doesn't matter that much.

12 Practice Space

Victoria looked as though she could not believe me.

"You played with a *pro*?" she said. "For real?"

I shifted a shoulder and deflected one of Willie's street-hockey shots. "He was really old," I said. "Fifty or something. He hasn't been a pro for twenty years or more."

"But he played pro!" she said, slamming her stick down.

"With P.J.," said Willie, like an echo.

"Not with P.J.," I said. "He plays in P.J.'s Thursday pickup game."

Willie flip-flapped the puck back and forth on his stick, preparing a shot.

"I didn't think P.J. was *that* good," he said.

"He's not," I said. I didn't know why I said that. I paused. "*Now* he's not. He's ... old. But Loney, the pro, said P.J. likely could have been a pro." I let them chew on that. After a pause, I added. "So he is good. For an old guy."

Victoria took a shot at me. I made a stick save.

"Okay, Mr. Smartie," she said. "Let's see how you play goal when you're sixty-three."

"Sixty-four," I said.

"Is he that old?" Willie asked.

I did some mental arithmetic. "Yeah. I guess. Prolly."

"You mean, 'probably'," said Victoria. When I shot her a look, she explained, "My coach doesn't like us mumbling. She makes us dress properly and speak clearly."

"I'm sure that prolly helps on the ice," Willie said, mumbling.

Victoria stuck out her tongue the way she used to do when we were ten. "I think your whole team sucks," she said. "They have P.J. as a coach but they don't know how lucky they are."

"You don't have to suffer through his skating drills," I said.

"Goalies have to be able to skate," she said. "Everybody has to be able to skate. It's a skating game."

"Huh," said Willie.

"Just look at the two of you," she said. "Your whole team. P.J. spends most of his time trying to figure out how to coach you guys, but none of you listen. You have a coach who is willing to put in the time. He's taking coaching courses. He talks to experts. He reads every book on coaching he can find. He's as crazy about coaching as you are about hockey."

Willie stood in awe.

"I didn't know about him taking courses and all that," I said. "And that other stuff. How do you know?"

Vickie looked at me like I was an insect. "Because he still comes out to some of my practices," she said. "Because he's the goalie coach for the Flames. And because when he tells me stuff, I listen. You ever try that?"

* * *

Grandpa Gord was awake when we visited him in the hospital that afternoon.

"How are you?" I asked, relieved to see him looking, well, normal.

"Able to sit up and take nourishment," he said, the twinkle in his eyes dimmed a bit but still there.

He still wore plastic mask over his face. The tubes and cuffs were still on his arm. The little TV monitor still showed the little spikes of his heartbeat.

"Don't you eat too much," said Nanny Joyce. "You're still not out of the woods."

"You mean I'm not dead yet," said Grandpa Gord, lifting his mask to talk. "And I don't plan on being for a while either."

He leaned back on his pillow and looked tired.

"Your team make first place yct?" Nanny Joyce asked.

The question surprised me.

"Why?"

"Didn't somebody mention a tournament in January? In Markham? And don't you have to be in first place for that?"

"Naw, somebody got that wrong. But if we win our game this weekend we can qualify." I didn't know she cared at all about hockey.

Nanny Joyce ran her hand over Grandpa Gord's forehead.

Grandpa Gord reached up and held her hand. He used his other hand to adjust his oxygen mask. *Like a goalie adjusting his face mask*, I thought.

"Now, don't you be getting excited," said Nanny Joyce. "You'll not be going to any January tournament."

I must have shown a trace of disappointment. Grandpa Gord lifted his mask once more. "She's talking about me, not you," he said.

There was an awkward pause.

"Well, somebody has to cheer for the lad and his buddies," said Grandpa Gord. "That's what grandparents are for."

I smiled.

"Thanks," I said.

As I turned to go, Grandpa Gord called me back. "Jake."

"Yes?"

"The fiddle." He looked up at Nanny Joyce. "You

tell him." The mask went back on.

One of Grandpa's shirts, with the yoke and frilly stuff, was draped over a chair. I ran my fingers through the frills around the yoke.

"Your grandfather thought he was feeling well enough earlier today to work on that shirt," said Nanny.

"On the shirt?" I asked, puzzled.

"He does his own embroidery on all his shirts," she said. "Did you know that?"

I looked up at my grandfather. He winked.

"Some things," he said, his voice muffled by the oxygen mask, "you have to do yourself."

Nanny said, "Remember that new fiddle the kids gave Grandpa for his birthday?"

It had only been five days before. "Yes, it's a beauty," I said.

Nanny Joyce said, "It was really great of the kids to spend all that money. Two thousand dollars for a fiddle. Can you imagine? But Gord told them he didn't want it."

I had seen it in his eyes at the party.

Grandpa Gord took off his mask. "I told the kids I wanted drums."

"Drums?" I asked.

"So they took the fiddle back and we're getting drums," said Nanny.

Grandpa Gord lay back on his pillow, smiling.

"A whole drum set," said Nanny. "For the music room. At our place."

"A drum set!" I said.

"A rock-and-roll drum set," said Grandpa Gord.

"Rock?" I said.

Nanny said. "Nice echo we have in here. We've got that practice room downstairs. Gord's band plays there. But when the drummer left, he took his drums with him. So we thought, if we had drums, Gord's band could still practice. And you could come over and practice. You and your band."

"Practice? With my band?" I asked.

Nanny put her hands on her hips. "Yes, practice. By yourself, or with your whole band. Any time you want, you could take the drums off to wherever you are playing."

"Or take them home, if you want," said Grandpa Gord. "But I don't think you've got the room."

"A rock drum set," I said, grinning so widely I felt silly.

"A rock drum set," Nanny said. "They'll be yours. We can keep them simply because we have the space — and a soundproof room."

Grandpa Gord said, "You can't have a rock band without drums. Drums keep the band together, drive the rhythm. Just like you do with your hockey team."

"A goalie like a drummer?" I said. What an idea!

"Hockey is a game of rhythm," Grandpa Gord said.

"Learning to time deflections. Taking passes. It's like jazz."

"You take it easy, Gord," Nanny Joyce said.

"It's the way I see the game. It's music," he said. "Not all goalies are like drummers. Some just stand there and try to stop pucks. But you set the pace. I've seen it. The others pick it up from you. Don't ever stop."

He rested his head back on the pillow.

"But what about …" I didn't know what to say.

"The kids?" said Nanny. "Your aunts and uncles? They're not kids any more. They can deal with it."

"I'm in hospital after a cardiac event," said Grandpa Gord, grinning. "What's the use of being a cranky old man if you can't just do what you feel is right rather than what other people want? If I can't do that now, then when?"

When, indeed.

"So practice hard," said Grandpa Gord.

"Practice," I said, aware that I must have sounded like an echo, a dumb echo.

"And good luck in your game," said Nanny.

"I likely won't be there to cheer you on," said Grandpa Gord, putting his mask back on.

"You *certainly* will not be there to cheer him on," said Nanny Joyce.

I hugged them both.

13 3H Hockey

The Roofers practiced that Friday evening. It was not a pretty sight.

In the dressing room you would have thought somebody died.

Usually it is quiet, with everyone plugged into their MP3 players. P.J. stopped to talk to several players. Each time he had to tap the person on the shoulder. Then the earphones would come out. P.J. would talk, giving out his coaching advice. Then the earphones would go back in.

I remember what Grandpa Gord had said about team rhythm. All these guys were listening to different music. I tried yelling to get everyone's attention. Nobody could hear me.

I didn't think the practice could be worse than the last one. Once we got on the ice, I could see it just might be.

P.J. tried to prod everybody to skate fast in his

drills. That did not work. Almost everybody dogged it. Several players still wore their earphones. They could not hear P.J.'s instructions, and had to just follow everybody else.

P.J. was getting frustrated. But after four laps around the rink to warm up, five more end-to-end skates, and then blue-line-to-blue-line stops and starts, he gathered everybody to one end of the rink.

"This isn't working, guys," he said.

Everybody shifted back and forth on their skates like NHLers "at attention" for the anthem. The silence was punctuated by distant echoes from the next ice pad.

"It can only work if you make it work," he said.

More silence. Everyone examined their skate laces.

"Sunday afternoon's game against the Cougars — a win will put us in the top three in the league. We can still qualify for the Markham tournament."

A few players looked up like kicked puppies.

"Fat chance of that," said Frank Kennedy.

"And I'll tell you what's more," P.J. said. "You won't have cowbells up in the stands to cheer you on."

I had a lump in my throat. I looked around and everybody was shifting their eyes in embarrassment.

"Here's what we're going to do," said P.J. "Whether or not it works depends on how much you put into it. I can't force you to skate hard in practice. But if you don't skate hard in practice, the other team will always run over you by the third period."

"Yeah," said Joseph.

"That's what happened the last two games," he said. "A couple of guys can't make it and you're down a line, then you need the legs."

Finally Frank said, "We tried our best."

"Of course you did. Nobody said you didn't. What we're after here is to make your best even better. That's what practice is for. So here's our drill. Jake, you head down to the far goal."

I waited to hear more.

"Don't wait. Go."

I did, gliding backward the last few feet into my goal crease.

At the far end, P.J. tooted his whistle. The team started to come at me. Joseph rushed out toward me. When he reached the blue line, he turned to skate backward. At the same time, two forwards started after. One of them picked up the puck that P.J. pushed out.

They were skating. Not very fast, but they were skating. Sort of.

Okay. I read the play — two on one. I hunkered down for the action.

But then a fifth player started out from the far end. It was the centre, but from P.J.'s shouts it was obvious his job was to back-check.

The forwards came but, before they could do anything, Frank broke up the play. The puck dribbled into the corner.

P.J. tooted his whistle again. Another defence set out; two more forwards came at him; a fourth back-checked.

Same deal, only this time Dylan got a pass to Bob Beattie, who in turn got away a weak shot. I kicked it out with my left pad.

Still, they were not skating hard. Not like they would in a game.

But already the next wave was coming my way. Two guys rushing me, one guy chasing them — over and over. When everyone had taken part in the rush exercise, P.J. gathered us around again.

"That's good, but you can do better. Here's the deal: if you're the back-checker, the fourth guy, you get three points if you touch the puck."

"Huh?"

"If you're the defence and you break up the rush, you get two points."

"But that's …"

"And if you're one of the rushing forwards, and either one of you gets a pass or a shot on goal, then you each get a point."

I think some of the team had to take off their hockey gloves to count the points.

"We have ten minutes to work on this," he said.

A few of the players began to show some interest.

"And after practice, I've got some treats for the top point-getters."

Now some others showed interest.

"Like, what kind of treats?"

P.J. shrugged. "Not much. Free pizza. A CD. Something like that. We'll call it the 3H Award."

"You mean 4H, don't you? That farm club," said Richard Hewitt, who had relatives who actually farmed.

"No, 3H," said P.J. "Happy, Hustle, Hurry — 3H."

He pulled a CD case from under his sweater. "Top point-getter owns this."

Fridg Fungus — the favourite of more than half the team. Now he had their attention.

It was a funny thing, that practice. Richard won the 3H Award. Until then, everybody thought he was one of the slowest on the team.

There was a bit of buzz in the dressing room afterward. But after P.J. gave out the CD and the pizza coupons, the earphones went back in.

It wasn't much for team spirit, but it was a start.

I knew something had to be done to kick this team back into the zone. I wasn't sure what it would take.

That night I talked it over with Willie. Then Willie called two players, and I called two players, and those players called two players, in a series that one of my grandfathers once said was like looking at your reflection in a mirror reflected in a mirror.

Then I called Jamie. Somebody had to.

"The team needs you," I told him. "I need you in

front of the net. We also need you to score a few goals."

Jamie listened. "But I don't think my dad ..." he said, his voice trailing off on the phone like a bad signal.

"This isn't about your dad," I said. "It isn't about my grandfather. It's about our team."

We were both silent for a moment.

"Our team," Jamie repeated.

"We have one chance now to tighten up," I said. "A coach can help. But if we really want to do it, nothing can stop us."

"Well ..."

"Otherwise, the whole hockey season won't be much fun. For anybody."

"But my dad ..."

"No, this is about you. Us. The team. The Roofers. Or if we're not the Roofers, maybe we're the P.J.s. We'll change our uniforms and play in our pyjamas." I was joking, kind of.

"I need my dad to drive me to the rink."

"If you want to play, you'll walk to the rink if you have to."

"I live in Bowmanville."

"Then we can pick you up. Are you in or out?"

There was another pause. Then, "What about the other guys?"

"We'll find out next game, won't we?"

Another pause.

"In or out?"

14 The Team Arrives

The whole team turned up early for the game. We were so early we had to stand in the hall outside the dressing room and wait for the previous team to get out.

"How's your grandfather?" asked Joseph. "He okay?"

"Which one was that?" asked Maurice. "I can never keep them straight."

"The one with the cowbells," said Joseph. "He had a heart attack, right?"

"It wasn't a bad one," I said. "He's going to be fine. He's coming home in few days."

Joseph slapped his stick against my goalie pads, which were draped over my shoulder. Why do players like to slap their sticks against goalie pads, whether or not the goalie is wearing them?

"We'll miss the cowbells," he said. "The whole team will."

Several other players who had been listening nodded in agreement.

"Me, too," I said. "Me, too."

P.J. arrived. He glanced from player to player, as though counting. His eyes came to rest on Jamie.

"I'm sorry?" P.J. said to Jamie, with a smirky grin. "I didn't get your name."

Jamie didn't flinch. "I'm sorry, too," he said. "I missed the last two games and the practices. I'd still like to be on your team."

Just like that.

P.J. didn't hesitate. "Not *my* team," he said. "*The* team. But next practice you'll have to serve a detention. Extra homework. Maybe block a few extra slapshots."

Willie stepped up. "I missed the last game, too," he said. "I'm sorry. My family had a holiday dinner."

"Okay," said P.J. "Your detention will be to take the slapshots that Jamie has to block. Then he'll do the same for you."

Willie was slow to smile. At last he caught on. "That'd be okay."

P.J. broke into a smile. "Just kidding both of you," he said. "You want to play, just be ready to skate."

Jamie looked at his skates. They were hanging over his shoulder, tied together with skate laces. "Just had them sharpened," he said.

"Both sides?" asked P.J.

Jamie looked puzzled. "What do you mean, 'both sides'?" he asked.

"You need them sharp on one side for rushing up the ice and sharp on the other for back-checking," replied P.J. "It's called two-way hockey."

"Oh," said Jamie, finally grinning. "Yeah. Sharp on both sides."

P.J. unlocked the dressing room door and our guys filed in.

P.J. stood by the door with Jamie for a half minute after everybody else had entered.

"What about your dad?" he asked.

"Don't know," said Jamie. "He doesn't know I'm here."

"I see." Which was good, because I didn't.

P.J. smiled and reached out to chuck Jamie under the chin.

Jamie glanced down at P.J.'s hand — just in time for P.J. to catch him with a tweak on the end of the nose.

"Skate fast and keep your head up," he said, and everybody laughed.

I plunked down the old boom box I had liberated from Fred. I found an electrical socket and plugged it in. Then I cranked it.

AC/DC blasted out, over-mod, assaulting every ear in the room.

"Okay, get those plugs out," Jamie yelled, pointing at Carl Biro, who tried to adjust his MP3 player.

"You, too, Frank," Willie added.

The message was clear. All the earphones came out.

"Do we have to listen to *this* stuff?" Carl asked.

"No," Richard said. "You win the 3H Award next practice and you get to call the play." He handed me a CD he had burned at home. I switched disks. Fridg Fungus rattled the coat hangers.

"3H Award?" said Jamie. "What's all that?"

Carl told Willie and Jamie about the practice.

I turned down the music just for a moment. P.J. held up his hands.

"Guys, guys. Guys."

Everybody focused on P.J.

"About the 3H award."

I looked around the room. They *were* interested.

"Same rules in the game," he said. "We're not after goals. We're after skating. Three points if you catch somebody back-checking. Two points for defence. One point for a shot on goal or assist on a goal."

Some of the players started counting on their fingers.

"Who's going to keep score on all these points?" asked Richard. "And don't we need goals to win?"

"Who is going to keep score of the points? You are."

"But what if ..."

"If someone pads his numbers? Cheats on his

teammates?" He let that one sink in.

"Richard's right," said Jamie. "We have to win this game."

"Goals count one point, the same as a shot on goal."

"But that's …"

"And we don't *have* to win this game. We would *like* to win this game. But more important is how you guys come together as a team. How you skate both ways. That you're Happy, you Hustle, and you Hurry."

"Hurry?" asked Willie. "Sounds like soccer."

"It is," said P.J. "I borrowed the idea from a soccer coach. 3H sounds better than HHS, Happy, Hustle, and Shoot. So it's Happy, Hustle, Hurry. We get more guys shooting on goal and we'll get more goals. Simple as that."

The message sank in.

"Okay, and today we play the Cougars," said P.J. "They're fast. But you knew that. And they have that Allrick kid."

"Old Lars!" said Jamie. "We'll get him."

"He's big, and he's fast, and he's strong. But he's only one guy. He puts on his hockey pants one leg a time." P.J. paused. "Of course, he can do it while he's stick-handling."

Another pause, and some guys even snickered.

"So one amendment for our 3H Award," he said, as though he was thinking this up on the spot. "Back-

check and catch Lars and you get double the points
— six. Okay?"

"Okay!" the team yelled.

"Everybody happy?"

"Happy!" we yelled back.

"Now crank that machine back up. Let's hear a little *team* here."

I thought that old CD player would bust a speaker.

15 A Happy Team

From the opening whistle, the team showed its happy face.

Dylan started off with a rush that surprised everyone, even Lars. I mean, *especially* Lars. Dylan just chipped the puck around him from the face-off, chased it, and in two strides was over the Cougars blue line.

Dylan has moves. Ryan says he got them playing street hockey. That's where you get to try all the silly things no coach would let you get away with.

Dylan headed straight for the Cougars goal. Both defence were waiting. No one else was around. Dylan's two wingers had been caught flat-footed and were still at centre ice. He had no one to pass to.

So the two Cougars defence closed in on him, aiming, I guess, at putting him in a vice. I braced myself for the crunch that I knew was coming.

It didn't happen like that. Dylan spun once, pushed

the puck ahead. As the two defence collided — and they did it with a crunch — Dylan danced around them and picked up the loose puck. He deked the goalie with a fake to the left, a deke to the right, and then a flip to the top shelf.

It was a pro move. Our bench exploded.

Up in the stands, Victoria and a half-dozen of her teammates on the Clarington Flames yelled and made so much noise you'd think they were having fun.

"*Roofers! Roofers! Roofers!*"

There was just one problem: scoring early on a team like the Cougars is like punching a bully in the nose. Right from the next face-off, the Cougars were *mad*.

Lars stayed on. So did Ryan. But this time Lars did not make the same mistake. He tangled with Ryan and used his size to make sure Ryan didn't go anywhere. Then he kicked the puck to his winger. The winger passed it back to the defence. The defence cruised forward, rushed along the right side, and dumped it in deep.

Simon Lee started back to dig the puck out of the corner to my left. P.J.'s skating drills made their mark. Instead of skating back carefully, he skated full speed, no hanging back.

The Cougar winger chased him. We had made them angry with speed, skill, and a bit of luck. Now they turned up their speed a notch, just when we turned up ours. I had the feeling that we were playing a different game.

Simon cleared the puck off the boards. Jamie picked it up and headed up-ice. He hit Ryan with a perfect pass just outside the Cougars blue line. In two steps, Ryan was in alone on goal again. This time he didn't try anything fancy. He just fired low and hard. I could hear the ring off the goalpost from my end of the ice.

The Cougars defence picked up the rebound. He hit Lars with a pass coming back. Lars did his patented full one-eighty. By the time he completed his turn, he was almost at our blue line. He came so fast our defence were on their heels trying to back up in front of him.

At the blue line, Lars deked just slightly to get around Simon. But Dylan had booted it back pretty fast. He caught Lars from behind. He couldn't get the puck from Lars. Lars was too good for that. But Dylan being there, right behind, forced Lars to lunge to the left to get away.

Lars' linemate on right wing hadn't expected this last move and had started in over our blue line. The linesman blew the play offside.

During the line change, I could see P.J. patting Dylan on the shoulder

For the whole first period, the Cougars kept coming at us. For the whole first period, the Roofers kept after them. When a Cougar went after a loose puck, our guys skated hard to try to beat them, even when they knew they didn't have a chance. They didn't give the Cougars a chance to make a play. Our guys forced them to make blind passes.

The clock for the period had begun to count down the last minute when Lars came back on. P.J. had been playing Dylan against Lars simply because he had the speed. But this time Lars came on with a line change on the go. He grabbed the loose puck at the centre-ice face-off circle and headed full-speed toward me, cutting to my left to get around Morley.

Morley skated with him, trying to ride him into the corner. In the meantime, Ted House came back. He caught Lars from behind and tried to pitch in around the outside.

Lars proved too strong for them both. Morley clung to his left, trying to force him to the outside. Ted squeezed him from the right, trying to grab the puck from him.

Lars forced his way through, dragging Ted from behind and carrying Morley almost over his left shoulder. He cut for the front of net. With no one to pass to, he came into my crease like a bulldozer. Once, twice, he shot the puck. Each time I kicked out a pad, felt the thump.

Then, on his way down, he got a third shot away that trickled through the five hole.

The first period ended with the score tied 1–1.

Between periods I skated to the bench for a drink.

★ ★ ★

"Way to go, guys," P.J. was saying. "Morley, don't forget your two points for that last play. You, too, Ted. Three points. You caught Lars."

"But he scored!" said Ted. "Isn't the idea to stop him from scoring?"

"You caught him," said P.J. "That's what counts. You keep catching him like that, you'll take away most of his chances. On that play he was just good, determined, and strong. That's not your fault."

When the second period started, by P.J.'s point system, we were winning the game hands-down. By the scoreboard, it was even. It didn't stay even very long.

Mostly it was Lars. Halfway through the period he came in again, just as he had the first time, dragging two players with him. Instead of shooting, though, he managed to kick a pass to his left. One of his wingers got to the puck before our defence could clear it. And before I could slide over. That made it 2–1.

With four minutes to go, Lars wound up behind his own net, made two nifty moves around our forwards, deked around our centre, left both our defence sprawled on the blue line examining their athletic supporters for jock itch, and walked in on me as though it was a shootout.

I stoned him.

With a left pad kick, I blocked his shot.

Lars fell. He came crashing into the crease.

I reached out to corral the puck. It squirted out of reach. Lars swung his stick from side to side, trying to knock it into the net.

Another Cougar arrived at the scene of the crash. I reached for the puck again. A stick came down on my glove hand.

Glancing up, I saw Jamie lift the Cougar off his feet.

Again I grabbed at the loose puck, but Lars was lying across my pads. I couldn't move.

And someone kept slapping with his stick at my glove hand as I tried to smother the puck.

Jamie stood his ground.

Finally, I lunged forward to cover the puck with my chest.

After an eternity, the whistle blew. I looked up to see the ref pointing straight down into the net.

Goal.

Desperately, I tried to make the no-goal sign. It couldn't be.

As the players tried to untangle their skates and sticks and legs and arms, I was able to get up on my knees. The puck was in the net. The score was 3–1.

Even with Jamie and Willie standing over me as enforcers, the Cougars had scored.

Worse was to come.

Less than a minute later, Lars broke through again. This time, he fired a slapshot halfway in from the blue line.

I caught it in my glove, but it was a hard shot and I couldn't hold it. The puck trickled out of my glove and into the corner of the net behind me.

4–1 for the Cougars.

16 Pull the Goalie

That's when P.J. made what the team thought was the dumbest coaching move they had ever seen.

He pulled me.

Me, the goalie. Me, Jake Henry, his own grandson.

Not to replace me with the backup goalie, either. He pulled me with four minutes to go for an extra attacker.

The team, you might say, was steamed. P.J. gathered them around the bench for a time-out.

"It's called a surprise," he said. "Now if you guys ever skated, this is the time. Dylan, pull out all the stops."

He looked at Jamie. "And you, Jamie. See if you can catch Ryan in the clear. Or set up Willie for his slap-shot. Watch for the breaks."

Willie looked around the rink. He looked up in the stands at the glum faces of moms and dads who were just dumbfounded as we were. "I wish the crowd would get into this game," he said.

"Where's your Grandpa Cowbells when you need him?" asked Jamie.

The ref tooted his whistle. Time to play. Our guys skated out for the face off.

Looking at the game from the bench sure was different. Looking at my empty goal was different.

The ref was just about to drop the puck. The rink went silent, with only quiet sounds deflecting from the cold metal rafters. Then came the sound of ringing cowbells.

They started in slow, like they did when Grandpa Gord was trying to carry them quietly. But they got louder and finally became so clear that even the ref straightened up and looked around.

From the sound, I could tell the cowbells came in from the far end of the rink. I could hear them mounting the stairs in the corridor. The ref held the face-off as everyone turned to follow the path of the sound. Finally, around the corner of the stairwell, Nanny Joyce appeared. She took a place at the spectator rail. Beside her was Grandpa Ron. Beside him was my father.

Nanny Joyce waved the cowbells over her head at me. I waved back.

The ref looked up at her. Then he looked at our bench. I nodded. With a toot on the whistle, the ref dropped the puck.

You'll never be able to tell me that the cowbells didn't help.

Jamie, playing centre for the first time that year, won the face-off.

Jamie got the puck back to Dylan, who was on defence. He had room to move, and used it. He rushed forward, deked twice, and headed over the Cougars blue line. He scooted down the boards, not even trying to cut in.

The Cougars right defence went after him. Or tried to go after him. But Dylan worked his way along the boards past the face-off circle. By this time the defence had committed himself. Dylan ragged the puck, twisted once, and lifted the puck around behind the net.

Jamie picked up the loose puck in the far corner. Dylan headed for the net. Willie drifted in from the point just inside the blue line. Jamie caught Dylan with a perfect pass; Dylan dropped the puck behind him to Willie, who cruised in to the face-off circle.

Willie let his slapshot go with full force. It rose high and went in over the Cougar goalie's left shoulder. He didn't even see it.

It was 4–2. The cowbells went wild.

Up in the crowd, my mother and Fred had joined Grandpa Ron and Dad around Nanny Joyce. As far as I knew, this was the first hockey game Nanny Joyce had ever seen. But she sure knew when to ring those cowbells.

By pulling me out of the net, P.J. had made sure of

one thing: the crowd was now into the game. Even the parents and family fans for the Cougars were buzzing. Who had ever heard of pulling a goalie in the second period?

Our guys were pumped. Well, maybe "frightened" was a better word. They knew that one mistake out there and the roof would cave in. Three-and-a-half minutes to go.

From the face-off, Jamie won again. This time Willie grabbed the puck. He simply dumped the puck into the Cougars end. Everybody chased it.

A Cougars defence scooped up the puck, but our forwards were rushing him. Without looking, he lifted the puck high toward our end of the rink.

The puck dropped past centre ice, behind our defence.

It did a little puck dance, wobbling on edge toward our goal.

Over the blue line, still wobbling.

Slowing down. Wobbling.

Gently it slid into the goal crease, *my* goal crease.

Then it slipped over the goal line, nicking the outside of the goalpost ever so slightly and spinning into the end zone.

Icing.

This gave us another face-off in their end of the rink.

From my strange seat on the bench, I could see

Nanny Joyce and my family. I could hear the gentle tinkling of the cowbells.

I could see my empty goal, and the clock with three minutes remaining in the period.

Toot.

Willie won the face-off.

He got the puck to Jamie; Jamie to Carl; Carl to Frank; and back to Willie, who got away a weak shot. But the goalie had been expecting one of Willie's cannons, and misplayed it. He bobbled the puck with both hands.

Dylan rushed in from the left side. With one swat, he batted the rotating puck with a knee-high swing of his stick into the net.

The score was 4–3. The cowbells clattered. Some in the crowd yelled and whistled and pounded on the railing.

We were back in the game. P.J. put me back in the net.

The second period ended. We knew the third would be a barn-burner.

★ ★ ★

From the face-off, the Cougars came charging back. Lars won the draw. He pulled the puck back to his defence, stepped around Dylan and took the perfect pass. He came straight down the centre.

I blocked the shot.

Jamie roared in and gave the loose winger a body-check that sent him into me. Both of them came down hard on me. Being at the bottom of a squirming, swearing pyramid isn't fun. I was on my back. The puck dribbled lazily six inches from my face. With my arms pinned, I couldn't reach it.

The puck moved toward the goal line. I turned on my left side and pulled my right arm free. I plunked my glove hand down over the puck.

And then the stick hit me hard, right on the knuckles. I thought my hand was broken.

Helplessly, I watched the puck dribble out of my glove and slide over the goal line.

Cougars danced on their skates in front of me, arms held high. Even the guy on the pile on top of me tried to raise his hands.

I ignored the yells from the crowd and the shrieking whistle. I got to my feet and skated over to the Cougar who had scored.

I pushed him. Startled, he rocked back on his heels.

Then I heard the shrill whistle of the referee. Jamie and Willie appeared, one on each side of me, holding me back.

"He chopped my hand," I said. "I want a piece of him."

The ref must have been making wild gestures then, because all of a sudden the crowd went quiet. Quiet, except for one, clear voice.

"Go get him, Jake!" yelled Nanny Joyce, waving the cowbells over her head. "He can't do that to you. Go get him."

I held my goalie stick like a club. I don't think I would have used it, at least not on purpose. I'm not sure, because I didn't have a chance.

I looked over at the ref. He had his arms straight out to each side in a gesture every goalie loves: No goal.

He repeated the gesture clearly three times, in case someone missed it. Then he whistled shrilly again and pointed at the Cougar I had almost assaulted. "Two minutes," he said, "for goalie interference." I could have kissed that ref.

Then he turned to me with another whistle blast and pointed an accusing finger. "You, two minutes for roughing."

It took the ref two minutes to settle everybody down. In one quieter moment I could hear Nanny Joyce. "Go get 'em, Jake!"

Eventually, the referee skated to the face-off circle to my right and we were ready to resume.

4–3 for the Cougars.

Three-and-a-half minutes left on the clock.

Four-on-four hockey.

* * *

P.J. called a time-out. We all went to the bench.

"Go for it," P.J. said. "We've got the advantage now, with fast skaters like Dylan and Ryan." To me he said: "Good move. It's about time you stood up for yourself."

He grinned and tried to tweak me under the chin. Considering I had a helmet and face mask on, that wasn't easy.

"When there's one minute to go, keep your eye on the bench. We still have a chance to tie this game. And listen, guys, clear it along the boards. Unless you're desperate, no icing."

Finally, to Jamie: "And whatever you do, don't clear it up the centre in front of your own net. It's too dangerous."

"And keep your stick on the ice!" said Willie.

It was now our game to win or lose.

Most of the next three minutes of hockey we should all forget. The Cougars, led by Lars with his power and skill, dominated us. The puck never left our end. Time after time, Lars simply powered his way to the goal. Once I kicked out with a pad save, once I used my blocker, twice I used my stick. Three times I poked-checked him on the crease. Only one Cougar came in my crease, though, and no one tried to dig a lose puck out of my glove.

Our guys skated hard, but just couldn't make it click. The play being in our end made it impossible for

P.J. to pull me. We had to get the play down to their end.

Dylan did manage that, with about thirty seconds left, intercepting a pass back to the point. But he was near the end of his shift. He got over centre ice, saw that the Cougars defence had put three players between him and the goal, so he simply dumped it in and went to the bench.

Jamie took his place and went flying into the Cougars end zone. The Cougar defence with the puck, surprised by Jamie being there, turned quickly to pass the puck. He lifted it high, straight up the centre, with all his forwards skating back toward him.

I glanced at the clock — twenty-nine seconds left. At the bench, P.J. was signalling me to come off.

The puck dropped to the ice at centre and headed toward me.

It was decision time. Should I continue to the bench, hoping the puck would miss the net and be called icing? That would bring the face-off back to the Cougars end.

Lars had turned and was using his full speed to head for the puck. I was way out of my net. If Lars beat me to it, the game was over.

I skated flat out to centre ice, racing Lars to the puck. I beat him, but just barely.

I got the puck at our blue line. I pulled it away from Lars. As hard as I could, I fired the puck to Jamie, who was just coming out of the Cougars zone. Then I sprinted to the bench. I didn't look back.

Willie jumped on for the extra attacker. I didn't take time to look until the bench gate had closed behind me.

Jamie had picked up my pass. He headed in, deked around one defence, then another. He shot from the top of the left face-off circle.

It was a hard, rising shot. The Cougars' goalie caught it with his left shoulder. It bounced high, turning over and over in the air.

By this time Willie was there. Before the puck even hit the ice, Willie slapped at it hard, at ankle level, just out of the crease.

He scored! The score was tied 4–4.

On the bench, we jumped up and down and danced and yelled. In the stands, our fans yelled and danced and jumped up and down. Cowbells rang. I looked up to see Nanny Joyce beaming, and wondered if she would come to another game, another time.

Later, I even got to see the official score sheet. It read: Third period: 19:47: ROOFERS: Westeweicz from Reisberry and Henry.

Henry, that's me. Jake Henry. With my first assist while playing goal.

17 Roofers Rage

After the game, Mr. Reisberry barged into the dressing room and marched right up to P.J. "You didn't make the Markham tournament, you know," he said.

P.J. looked him in the eye. "I know," he said, not blinking. "And we tied a team we should have beaten."

"But that's neither here nor there," Mr. Reisberry said, holding out his hand. "You've done a great job with these guys. That was a great game. This sponsor's back, and we're going to have a season to remember."

He gripped P.J.'s hand and held it.

"Hear that, guys?" P.J. said. "Don't bring your pyjamas to the next game. You're still Roofers." P.J. and Jamie's father laughed together and shook hands .

"But you have to know," P.J. said, "that these guys brought themselves together. And that's a hundred times better."

"If we can help them enjoy themselves, and teach them to rely on themselves to get things done, we'll be happy," said Mr. Reisberry.

Grandpa Ron came through the door quietly. I didn't know he was there until he was standing right in front of me. Behind him was my dad.

"Look who I dragged along," he said.

"Great game!" said Dad. "Looks like we've got a bit of catching up to do." He paused. "We stopped off at the hospital to see your granddad. He's doing fine. How'd you like the passenger we picked up?"

"Nanny? That was great. The whole team loved it."

P.J. interrupted with his big voice.

"Now listen everybody," he said. "Great Game. To celebrate, we're going out for pizza."

The team cheered.

P.J. raised both hands. "And Saturday, after practice," he said, "I want to treat you all to a visit to *Total Hockey* at the Rickard Arena. You can all measure the speed of your slapshots."

"What if Willie breaks the machine?" asked Jamie, and everyone laughed.

It was a dressing room filled with shouts. I cranked up the CD player.

P.J. suddenly appeared right beside me. He reached down and rumpled my hair as though I were six.

"Not bad, Jacob Henry, not bad. You're getting the hang of things. You start your own band, you clear your own crease. And now you set up a tying goal. Next thing you know, you'll score a goal."

I looked over at Jamie and Willie. Together we laughed.

"We'll work on that," I said.

Other books you'll enjoy in the Sports Stories series

Ice Hockey

❏ *Deflection!* by Bill Swan

Jake and his two best friends play road hockey together and are members of the same league team. But some personal rivalries and interference from Jake's three all-too-supportive grandfathers start to create tension among the players.

❏ *Misconduct* by Beverly Scudamore

Matthew has always been a popular student and hockey player. But after an altercation with a tough kid named Dillon at hockey camp, Matt finds himself number one on the bully's hit list.

❏ *Roughing* by Lorna Schultz Nicholson

Josh is off to an elite hockey camp for the summer, where his roommate, Peter, is skilled enough to give Kevin, the star junior player, some serious competition, creating trouble on and off the ice.

❏ *Home Ice* by Beatrice Vandervelde

Leigh Aberdeen is determined to win the hockey championship with a new, all girls team, the Chinooks.

❏ *Against the Boards* by Lorna Schultz Nicholson

Peter has made it onto an AAA Bantam team and is now playing hockey in Edmonton. But this shy boy from the Northwest Territories is having a hard time adjusting to his new life.

❏ *Delaying the Game* by Lorna Schultz Nicholson

When Shane comes along, Kaleigh finds herself unsure whether she can balance hockey, her friendships, and this new dating-life.

❏ *Two on One* by C.A. Forsyth

When Jeff's hockey team gets a new coach, his sister Melody starts to get more attention as the team's shining talent.

❏ *Icebreaker* by Steven Barwin

Gregg Stokes can tell you exactly when his life took a turn for the worse. It was the day his new stepsister, Amy, joined the starting line-up of his hockey team.

❏ *Too Many Men* by Lorna Schultz Nicholson

Sam has just moved with his family to Ottawa. He's quickly made first goalie on the Kanata Kings, but he feels insecure about his place on the team and at school.

Skateboarding

❏ *SK8ER* by Steven Barwin

Jordy Lee and his friends are thrilled when a new skateboarding park opens in their neighbourhood, offering a competition with a prize. The talented Alisha might be able to coach Jordy to a win, but what will his friends think about him taking advice from a cute girl?

Track and Field

❏ *Mikayla's Victory* by Cynthia Bates

Mikayla must compete against her friend if she wants to represent her school at an important track event.

❏ *Fast Finish* by Bill Swan

Noah is fast, so fast he can outrun anyone he knows, even the two tough kids who wait for him every day after school.

❏ *Walker's Runners* by Robert Rayner

Toby Morton hates gym. In fact, he doesn't run for anything — except the classroom door. Then Mr. Walker arrives and persuades Toby to join the running team.

❏ *Mud Run* by Bill Swan

No one in the S.T. Lovey Cross-Country Club is running with the pack, until the new coach demonstrates the value of teamwork.

❏ *Off Track* by Bill Swan

Twelve-year-old Tyler is stuck in summer school and banned from watching TV and playing computer games. His only diversion is training for a triathlon race … except when it comes to the swimming requirement.

Soccer

❏ *Lizzie's Soccer Showdown* by John Danakas

When Lizzie asks why the boys and girls can't play together, she finds herself the new captain of the soccer team.

❏ *Alecia's Challenge* by Sandra Diersch

Thirteen-year-old Alecia has to cope with a new school, a new stepfather, and friends who have suddenly discovered the opposite sex.

❏ *Shut-Out!* by Camilla Reghelini Rivers

David wants to play soccer more than anything, but will the new coach let him?

❏ *Offside!* by Sandra Diersch

Alecia has to confront a new girl who drives her teammates crazy.

❏ *Heads Up!* by Dawn Hunter and Karen Hunter

Do the Warriors really need a new, hot-shot player who skips practice?

❏ *Off the Wall* by Camilla Reghelini Rivers

Lizzie loves indoor soccer, and she's thrilled when her little sister gets into the sport. But when their teams are pitted against each other, Lizzie can only warn her sister to watch out.

❏ *Trapped!* by Michele Martin Bossley

There's a thief on Jane's soccer team, and everyone thinks it's her best friend, Ashley. Jane must find the true culprit to save both Ashley and the team's morale.

❏ *Soccer Star!* by Jacqueline Guest

Samantha longs to show up Carly, the school's reigning soccer star, but her new interest in theatre is taking up a lot of her time. Can she really do it all?